Violets Are Blue
More Trouble Brews

Janet McNulty

Violets Are Blue More Trouble Brews

Copyright © 2017 Janet McNulty
Cover Illustration by Robert Henry

ISBN-10: 1-941488-75-7 (MMP Publishing)
ISBN-13: 978-1-941488-75-1

Library of Congress Control Number: 2017910566

Printed in the United States of America

To all those who did something fun on a lark.

Violets Are Blue
More Trouble Brews

Chapter 1

The toasty sun warmed me as I wandered through the maze of booths, each selling the owners' various talents: three-layer cakes, homemade ice cream, wood carvings, paintings, self-published books, glass figurines, hand-sewn quilts, and small flower pots filled with dirt and a packet of seeds in the center. Flamboyant music played in the background, filling the park with the sounds of patriotic tunes, making the atmosphere match the day. Glad to have the day off, of course Mr. Stilton usually closed the Candle Shoppe on the fourth of July anyway, I meandered among the booths, admiring the red, white, and blue trimmings that decorated each one.

A wooden teddy bear on a nearby table caught my attention and I picked it up, twirling it in my fingers, admiring the craftmanship and the time and effort put into creating its more delicate features. I placed the figurine back in its spot and moved on.

"Hey," said Jackie, walking up to me with a quilt she had just purchased.

"I thought you said that you weren't going to spend any money today," I chided her.

"You know me," she smiled, holding up the hand-made quilt.

Yep. I knew her. She never could resist a good buy, but Jackie had the means to pay for it.

"Where's Greg?" she asked.

"He said he would meet us here after he got off work."

I paused by the table with the books and picked one up, turning it over so that I could read the back cover description.

Learn about some of the oldest families in the state of Vermont, one of which is the Beaumontt family. Jean Beaumont originally immigrated from France in 1715 and bought a small plot of land that he used to create a successful business. Study and explore this unique family history of a Colonial family, and others, who lived in this humble state.

I put the book back down.

"Are you interested in local history?" asked the man attending the booth, who I assumed was the author.

"Not really," I said.

"That's a shame." He took his reading glasses off as

he placed the puzzle book he had been working on down. "Most people aren't, thinking that history should only consist of world-changing events, but it's usually the happenings in your local community that affect you the most."

I just smiled at him and continued on, not wanting to get involved in some deep conversation about local events. For now, I just wanted to enjoy the rest of the day, knowing that a giant backyard cookout awaited me at Tiny's. My mouth watered as I thought about the chicken and ribs soaked in BBQ sauce that I anticipated eating. Jackie hoisted her quilt, readjusting her hold on it and shifting it to her other arm as we walked.

"You can go put that in the car if you want," I told her.

"Nope. I'm good," she replied. "Oh, funnel cake!"

Jackie bee-lined for the funnel cake stand, her quilt flapping beside her as she ran and whipping people as she passed them.

"Hey!" shouted one woman, but Jackie ignored her, remaining focused on the cakes in front her that had come fresh out of the fryer, stopping only when she reached the table.

"How many?" asked the man behind the table.

"One," said Jackie, her mouth salivating for the cake, probably tasting it already.

"Two," I corrected her, running up beside her and wondering how she managed to beat me to the booth, considering that she carted that giant quilt that must have been hurting her arms by now.

The man gave us sidelong glance before turning and picking up the cup with the batter in it, pouring it into the fryer in a squiggly pattern. The smell of the cooking batter proved to be too much for Jackie as she licked her lips, imagining what her treat would taste like. Once done, he pulled the cakes out of the fryer, placing them on paper plates and sprinkled some powdered sugar on them.

"Any toppings?" he asked.

"Strawberry," said Jackie.

"The same," I replied when he looked at me.

He scooped a big heaping spoonful of strawberry topping and poured it all over the two cakes while Jackie's mouth watered as she watched it drip down the sides and she snatched it, not even bothering to wait for him to hand the plate to her. She snatched it from the table and dug into her funnel cake. I took mine with a little more dignity, thanking the man, before picking mine up and taking a huge mouthful. Strawberry topping trickled down the side of my chin, having escaped the corners of my mouth.

"You didn't save any for me?" said Greg, walking up to us with a smile on his face.

I glanced down at my empty plate that had nothing more than a little dollop of the strawberry topping. Okay, so perhaps I was no better than Jackie when it came to eating funnel cake. I probably could eat several of those in one sitting, which is why I try to avoid them. "I saved you some strawberry glaze," I said, holding the plate out to him.

He smiled and took the plate, throwing it in one of the nearby trash cans before glancing at Jackie.

"Don't look at me," she said, still licking her fingers, "You can get you own."

Greg laughed.

"Here." Jackie thrusted the paper plate at him and he took, disposing of it in the same garbage can.

"I can get you one, if you want"—I handed him some money, but he turned it down.

"I just ate."

Jackie took the cash from my outstretched hand. "I can stand to eat another."

The squeal of a microphone pierced my ears and I turn around with everyone else to see who had stepped on the stage, which I hadn't paid much attention to, to speak to the crowd.

"Ladies and gentlemen," said a man, dressed in an ostentatious outfit complete with a gold-trimmed belt and pearl buttons lining the front of his yellow and green shirt, "let us say hello to the Fourth of July in the Park Pageant ladies!"

A few cheers went up in the crowd, but they seemed sparse and unenthused as people were more interested in the games and upcoming water fight.

"What's going on?" asked Jackie, munching on another funnel cake, this time it had caramel topping drizzled all over it.

"Some pageant," replied Greg.

"Oh, I heard about this," she said over a mouthful of cake. "It's kind of the precursor to the Miss Belle pageant which takes place later this week. It's a three-night event and anyone can join."

"So, what is the point of this one?" asked Greg.

"Probably just a way for the participants of the Miss

Belle to show their stuff and get some votes. It seems that if you win this, you have a good chance to win the other, and I overheard someone talking about how they do this just for fun."

Curious about the pageant in the park, I stepped closer to watch a group of women in their late teens and early twenties parade across the stage in their summer dresses all smiling and waving, looking sweet and charming. A part of me wondered if they all were as charming as they appeared.

"Give it up for Miss Jeanette Hensley," said the announcer.

A woman with reddish-blonde hair strutted across the stage in a rose-pink sun dress, waving at the crowd.

"Thank you," the announcer said. "And now we have Miss Diana Pinkett."

A woman in a red, white, and blue dress walked across the stage in an elegant fashion, doing what I have heard referred to as the beauty wave before going down the steps on the other end and disappearing into a group of tents, which I assumed served as the changing area.

The announcer introduced a few more women before we got to the last one. "And last, but certainly not least, is Miss Melanie Sanders."

"Mel!"

Oh no. I knew that voice. I glanced at Jackie and she and I shared a look of dread as we both recognized the shrill voice that screamed over the crowd, drowning out the announcer on the stage.

"Mel!"

I turned away, hoping that she would go away, but

knew that it was hopeless. It's bad enough that I have to see her each day at work, but can't I get away from her when I'm trying to enjoy myself at a town event?

"MEL!"

Tammy slammed into me, knocking me off my feet and to the ground, while Jackie sidestepped, avoiding the entire incident, and managing to shove the last piece of her funnel cake into her mouth. Of course, all I saw was a blur of bright red with white frills swaying from the hem of her skirt. Greg helped me up, allowing me to get a better look at my assailant and I noticed that to complete her outfit, Tammy had taken a blue tank top and bedazzled it with an array of sequins, all varying shades of red, in an effort to mimic what I can only assume is supposed to be fireworks, but it looked more like someone had vomited all over it.

"Didn't you hear me calling to you?" Tammy asked.

"If she didn't, everyone else did," mumbled Jackie.

"I didn't think I would meet you all here," Tammy said.

"And yet, here we all are," snipped Jackie.

"We do like to go out and enjoy our Fourth of July holiday like everyone else," I told Tammy.

"But I thought you would be solving a murder," Tammy said so loud that the people standing closest to us gave us sidelong glances.

"Not so loud," I hissed.

"In case you haven't been paying attention," Jackie said, "there is no murder to solve."

Tammy ignored Jackie's curt response and turned to Greg. "Oh, I see you brought your boyfriend with you."

Why she said this with surprise confused me, but this is Tammy after all. She isn't always the sharpest knife in the block.

"She occasionally lets me out of my cage," Greg joked and I playfully jabbed him with my fist in an effort to tell him to not egg her on.

"It's fiancé, actually," I told her.

Tammy's cheeks bulged as she clamped her mouth shut in an effort to contain her building excitement, but as her face turned a deeper shade of red and a low whistle escaped from her lips, I knew we were in for it. "OOOOO—Oh my gosh!" she squealed and more people turned our way as she jumped up and down shaking my arm and jiggling me to the point where I thought I would turn into literal jelly. "Congrats you two! When did that happen! I'm going to plan your bachelorette party."

"Ah, no," said Jackie. "That's my job."

"I thought she knew about our engagement," Greg whispered to me.

"I thought so too," I replied. "At least, I thought I had told her."

"It wouldn't matter if you had," Jackie said. "She has the memory of a squirrel."

"And now for the interviews," said the announcer, breaking up our conversation and I realized that we had missed most of this mini pageant.

I shushed Tammy and pointed at the stage, interested in who would win this little beauty contest. One by one, the man on the stage called the girls forward and asked them two questions, mostly ranging on politics or how they would solve one of the world's problems.

"Melanie Sanders," the announcer said, approaching a woman wearing an ocean blue dress, it's sequined top shone in the bright sunlight while its tulle skirt waved in the warm summer breeze. She tugged a bit at a sheer, matching blue scarf that she had draped around her neck in an effort to complete her outfit.

"Miss Sanders?" the announcer prodded when she did not answer.

The young woman wavered on her feet and her face had gone pale. She tried to speak, but the words coming out of her mouth were inaudible and faded. The more she struggled, the more I realized that the sweat on her face was not from standing in the hot sun.

"Greg," I said, "I think she's going to faint!"

Greg rushed to the stage to catch her as the woman collapsed in a crumpled heap to a mixture of shocked screams and gasps. He knelt by the woman, but shook his head as he checked her pulse. "Get these people away," he told the announcer and together, with the help of a few others in the crowd, they shooed the curious onlookers away. While they busied themselves with the crowd, I crept up to the woman and examined her sweaty face and noticed a scar on her neck. Hadn't she just been wearing a scarf? Searching the area, I meandered around the stage, trying to locate the missing scarf, but found nothing, concluding that perhaps it had fallen off and got swept away in the commotion.

"The police are on their way," Greg said, walking up to me. "What's wrong?" he asked when he noticed me looking for something.

"I'm trying to find her scarf," I said.

"Was she wearing one?" Greg asked.

The more I thought about it, the more I could not remember and the approaching police cars made it difficult to concentrate. My phone binged. I glanced at it, having a sneaky suspicion of who had texted me and when I read the message, my intuition proved to be correct.

I know you are there. Just stay where you are.

"Anything wrong?" Greg asked.

"Nope," I replied. "It's just Detective Shorts, and he knows exactly where to find me."

Jackie joined us a minute later and I told her what the detective had texted me. Out of the corner of my eye, I saw Tammy jumping up and down, waving at me in an effort to get through the gathering crowd and the police who had arrived, attempting to keep people away from the body. Jackie noticed her as well. She motioned for us to move elsewhere in an effort to avoid Tammy's buoyant personality and her insistence that we solve this latest mystery, but even I had to admit that perhaps the woman had died from the heat.

"I wouldn't worry about her," I whispered to Jackie, responding to her concerns about Tammy. "Detective Shorts is here."

We watched as the familiar four door car drove up and parked, sporting a few extra scratches and dings compare to what it had a few months ago. The detective parked the car and stepped out of the vehicle, wearing his typical thrift store suit, including the jacket, despite the 90-degree heat, and walked straight up to us, after taking a minute to be briefed by an officer.

"Miss Summers," he said to me in his usual straight-laced and no-nonsense tone, "this is becoming a habit of yours."

"Becoming?" said Jackie. "I think by now it is a habit."

I gave her a sidelong glare and she mouthed the word "what" to me.

Detective Shorts pulled out his notepad and pen and waited for us to speak, guessing by now that we knew the drill.

"Why don't you ever use your phone?" Jackie asked, allowing her curiosity to get the better of her. "It has a fancy little record function."

The detective scowled at her.

"Okay, well," said Jackie, dropping her inquisitiveness, deciding it best to answer his questions, "we were all standing over there, watching the pageant with everybody else when the woman…"

"You mean the victim?" asked the detective.

"Yes. When the victim crossed the stage, she collapsed and that was it."

"And you two?" Detective Shorts pointed at Greg and me.

"We ran up to check on her," Greg replied.

"Together?"

"No," I replied. "He checked the woman, while I stood by him and watched."

Detective Shorts arched his right eyebrow at me, not believing my statement that I did nothing but stand by Greg's side while he checked the victim's pulse. "Are you sure?"

"I was with him the entire time."

"Did you notice anything unusual?" he asked me.

"Just a scar on her neck," I replied, "and her scarf is missing."

"Scarf?"

"Yes. She had been wearing a scarf while on the stage."

"Did either of you notice if the victim had been wearing a scarf?" the detective asked Jackie and Greg.

Both of them shook their heads, muttering the word no and a few inaudible sentences, which conveyed that they did not remember.

Detective Shorts closed his notepad and shoved his pen back in his pocket. "I shouldn't have to remind you of this, but I am going to anyway"—he looked at me when he said this—"but do not get involved in this. Let the police handle it."

We all nodded our heads, signaling our compliance.

"Hey!" shouted Tammy, waving her arms in a frantic manner. "Hey, detective! Do you know who did it?"

Detective Shorts stopped and glared at her. "Excuse me?"

"Do you know who killed her?" Tammy asked, stopping in front of him, wheezing from all the physical exertion she had put herself through in trying to get our attention.

"This is an ongoing investigation," replied the detective.

"Come on. You must have a clue," Tammy begged him. "I can help you. Maybe she had some dirt on the other contestants and someone decided to get rid of her before she could blackmail them. Or perhaps she was in the witness protection program and—"

"Have a good day," Detective Shorts said in a curt voice, cutting Tammy off and walked away, ignoring her as she chased after him, spouting one theory after another. After two more minutes of her incessant badgering, he had an officer escort her from the premises.

"You're not really going to stay out of this are you?" Jackie asked me in a low whisper.

"For now, yes, at least, until I have something more to go on," I told her as I questioned my own eyes and what I thought I had seen when the woman collapsed.

A series of beeps performing their own piece of musical art caught my attention and I glanced in their direction just as Greg finished up with his phone and put it back in his pocket. "Just texting Jack, asking him to let us know what the coroner finds out when he files his report."

"What makes you think he will…"

"Oh, he will," replied Greg.

I smiled at him and glanced at the clock on my phone. "We should go."

Jackie and Greg agreed, and together, we all snuck away before Tammy noticed.

Chapter 2

The curtains of my window moved a little from the breeze in the gray daylight of the cloudy morning that chose to greet me when I woke up. I had cracked my window open before going to bed for a little bit of fresh air to get rid of some of the staleness of my room. I glanced at the clock. Still three hours to go before I had to be at work.

I opened up my laptop and typed in my pin to bring up my home screen before opening a web browser. After a few search attempts, I managed to find some results for yesterday's incident.

July 4th Pageant Murdered

Cute. Very cute. That's a good way to sensationalize someone's demise. I read some of the other search results.

Woman Dies of Heat Stroke
Pageant Contestant Collapses, July Fourth
Fourth in the Park Ruined by Sick Pageant Contestant
Last Heir of Vermont Dead
Police: Still No Word about Mysterious Death of Woman
in July 4th Pageant.

I clicked on the second from the top search result and read the single paragraph blurb.

Yesterday, during the mini-pageant in the Fourth in the Park event, a contestant by the name of Melanie Sanders collapsed on the stage and died shortly after. Though the police have yet to release an official report, it is believed that she might have succumbed to heat stroke. It was unusually warm that day and the temperature, mixed with the stress and costumes of the pageant, may have caused her to collapse.

As a reminder, the summer months are hot and people should be sure that they drink plenty of water and stay hydrated. If you feel yourself becoming…

I stopped reading the article when it went into a lecture about how to stay healthy and avoid the dangers of heat stroke or exhaustion. I scanned the list of results again and clicked on the one about the lost heir.

Yesterday, during the Fourth in the Park event, a woman named Melanie Sanders died of an apparent heat stroke. The state of Vermont is saddened by this loss as Miss Sanders was rumored to be the last of the Beaumonts. The Beaumonts are an old family and it is believed that Miss Sanders was the last of their line. Her untimely death is unfortunate as it means that their line has now ended.

I closed the page. A woman has died and all the author of this article cared about was that it meant the end of some old family line. A few drops of rain hit my window and I pulled the curtain back to look outside at the darkening clouds and frowned. Rainy days usually meant it would be slow at work.

Work…

Oh my gosh! I'm late! I looked at my clock and realized that I had wasted two and a half hours in front of my computer, researching yesterday's unfortunate event. I shut my laptop closed and rushed out of my room while hopping on one foot as I tried to get a shoe on. Jackie stood in the kitchen, sipping a cup of coffee.

"Hey, do you want some?" she asked me.

I stopped and looked at her with strands of my hair in my face and a dumbfounded expression.

"You're late again." Jackie picked up a To-Go cup—we had purchased a pack of 50 of them at the local Walmart for just this occasion—and filled it with some coffee, handing it to me.

"Thanks," I said.

"Oh, Greg stopped by as he left for work," she called after me, "and said that he will see you tonight."

"Thanks!" I waved good-bye to her and ran out the door, charging down the steps to the parking lot.

Traffic was light, which made me glad because I did not want to get stuck in it, and managed to make it to the Candle Shoppe just in time. I squeaked through the door and clocked in just before Mr. Stilton had a chance to notice my tardiness. After putting my bag in my locker in the back room, I straightened my shirt, preparing to head out to the main store area, but stopped.

A piece of delicate material stuck out of one of the lockers and I reached for it, allowing it to thread through my fingers, remarking at the unique flower pattern on it. The scarf. I knew that Melanie had been wearing a scarf. At least, I was certain of it, even though no one else remembered seeing her with one. As I studied the floral pattern with its softly blended yellows, blues, and greens, racing footsteps attacked my ears, telling me that I was about to get an unexpected surprise.

"Mel!" Tammy pulled me aside, ripping my hands away from the piece of cloth that poked out of a locker. "Who do you think did it?"

I gave her a dumbfounded look.

"Who do you think murdered that woman?"

"Tammy, I don't know and…"

"What have you got to go on? Where do you plan to start looking? Who struck you as the most suspicious person there yesterday?"

"Right now, you are acting a little suspicious," I told her, noticing a note on the white board in the back, saying that the shelf where our packages of scented wax for our wax warmers were needed to be restocked.

"What do you mean?" Tammy demanded, following

me around as I scooped up a couple of boxes with our scented wax and walked to the main store front.

"Well, I've only been here for a minute and already you want to know what I think about what happened yesterday at the park," I said as I plopped the boxes down on the carpeted floor and started to rearrange the packages of wax. "One could say that you have something to hide."

"Why—I'd—how dare you accuse me—"

"Tammy!" I hissed at her as her voice rose in pitch and volume with every word and a few customers peeked in our direction. "Keep it down."

"Well, you were accusing me of…"

"I wasn't accusing you of anything," I said to her. "Look, I was just trying… Never mind."

"So," Tammy insisted on pursuing the conversation, "what are you going to do?"

"What makes you think I'm going to do anything?" I asked her as I pulled some strawberry scented wax off the shelf, that had somehow got put with the hazelnut section, and put them back where they belonged.

"You are the local detective around here."

I stopped my task. "What do you mean?"

"Come on, Mel. Everyone knows that you are the one who solves the difficult cases that the cops can't. Remember the circus?"

Yes, I did. A few months ago, a traveling circus had come to town and one of the performers was murdered. Tammy had learned of my little investigation and had insisted on tagging along, almost botching the entire thing when she stole a tiger. I did not want a repeat of that.

"Tammy," I said, as I organized the shelf in front of me, "I am just going to let the police handle this one."

"What!"

More people looked our way. "Keep it down," I told her, motioning at a couple that strolled past us.

"But you have to do something."

"No, I don't. I'm not sure what happened and this time I am going to let Detective Shorts handle it."

"Even if they missed something?" Tammy asked in a sweet voice, and I should have known she was up to something, since she, like everyone else, knew my natural curiosity a little too well.

"What do you mean?"

"Well," began Tammy, settling in to hook me with her bait, "while you all were being questioned by the detective, I overheard some of the officers talking."

"Talking?"

Okay. Oaky. I know I should have known better than to fall for this, but Jackie always said that my propensity to want to figure things out tended to overrule any common sense I might have had.

"Yeah, they…"

"You know what? Never mind," I cut Tammy off at the last minute. "I don't want to know. I should start acting like the average citizen who does not get involved in—"

"The police found something in a culvert!" Tammy blurted out just as a woman with a basket of merchandise walked up to us, her eyes widening at the mention of police and culvert.

"May we help you?" I asked the woman.

She stared at us for a moment before holding out a battery-operated wax warmer that was supposed to be hung on a wall. "I think this is broken."

I stepped closer to take a look and noticed that the mechanism that attached to the wall had broken. "I will get you another one from the back," I said to her. "Do you want the same color?"

The woman nodded and the sound of someone clearing their throat grabbed my attention. "Tammy, will you help him?" I asked her.

A wave of disappointment crossed her face. I arched my eyebrows in response, hoping that she would understand my unspoken message: this is a store and we are employees here, which meant putting our conversation aside to help the customers. She released a puff of air and stalked over to the man in question while I went to the backroom with the wall warmer. Once I got there, I grabbed a form from the filing cabinet for returning a defective product and filled it out, marking down the serial number, color, and what the specific defect was, before packing it away in a box to return to the seller we had purchased it from.

The bell on the door binged and I looked up to see two more people come in. It seemed a bit odd to have so many people here so early in the morning and the day after a holiday. I returned to my task, sealing the package and dropping it in the "to be mailed" bin. After I had finished, I strolled over to where the other wall warmers were kept and pulled the box off the bottom self, and rifled through it, looking for another in the exact color as the one I had just marked as defective. Found one! Snatching it and heaving the box back on the shelf, I rushed out of the storeroom and back to the customer, whom I found standing by the cash register.

"You're in luck," I said to her. "I found another one in the same color."

She smiled, pleased that I had been able to help her.

"Will this be everything for you?" I asked her as I took the basket from her and rung up her items.

"Yes," she said.

I wrapped her delicate items in brown paper to help prevent them from breaking on the way home. "That will be fifty-six dollars and thirty-two cents."

She handed me a credit card and I swiped it, giving her a receipt to sign.

"Thank you," I said to her when she gave me back the receipt, snatching her bag of purchases and left.

A brief thought about where Tammy had gone to skipped through my mind just as I heard a slow creak. I looked up. Was that set of shelves tipping over? All we had were free-standing industrial shelves filling most of the store, with only some them attached to the wall, and the set in question leaned further and further. Before I had a chance to say anything, it toppled over. I watched, helpless, as it crashed into the set of shelves next to it, forcing it to fall over and plow into the set beyond it. One by one, the shelves closest to the register crashed into one another like a bunch of gigantic dominoes until the last one hit the floor with a resounding—*THUD!*

In the only rounded out bit of clear space, stood

Tammy with her knees squished together and a frightened look on her face. I glanced around. As the dust settled, and when my heart stopped beating to the point where I thought it would burst from my chest, I took note of the customers standing frozen in the store, afraid to move. Coming back to my senses, I ran to the fallen shelves, looking under them as best I could to make sure that no one had gotten caught underneath them. I breathed a sigh of relief. I did not want to have to call an ambulance.

"I… I…" Tammy struggled to find the words she searched for. "I was just trying to help you stock those warmers." Her low voice forced my ears to strain to hear her.

A couple of people walked out, dumping their items by the door. I had to think fast before everyone left and news got out about another mishap at the Candle Shoppe.

"I can help all of you over here," I said, pointing at the register. "I do apologize for all this. It looks as though the legs on one of our shelves buckled."

A couple approached me in slow motion, unsure if they could trust my words, or if something else might fall over. The woman handed me the two items she wished to buy, but her hands shook so much that her boyfriend had to take them from her and give them to me, while putting a reassuring arm around her shoulders.

Mr. Stilton stormed out of his office. "What is…" He stopped the moment he noticed me trying to help the remaining people in the store finish their purchases and clamped his mouth shut, but by the way the singular vein in his temple pulsed, I knew Tammy and I were in for it once the store cleared out.

"That will be twenty-two dollars and fifty cents," I said to the couple, wrapping their items. The boyfriend handed me twenty-five dollars and I gave him back his change. "Have a nice day!" I said to them as they left, realizing just how awkward my automatic farewell was at the moment.

Another man approached and I rung up his purchases, wrapped them up, and wished him a good day. For the next ten minutes, I took care of the customers who chose to remain and complete their shopping while Tammy hunkered near the disaster area, chewing on her nails while taking a few odd glances at Mr. Stilton's face and its darkening shade of red. When the last person stepped out the door, Mr. Stilton locked it, flipping the open sign to the side that said closed.

"What happened?" he asked, enunciating each word.

We looked at Tammy and she squirmed under our gaze.

"I… uh…" Tammy fiddled with her jeans and for the first time I noticed them. They were normal. No sequins, no bedazzling, no outrageous embroidering or colors. They were just a normal pair of blue jeans. "I just wanted to help Mel put the wall warmers away because she got called away to help a customer and the shelf just fell over."

"All of them?" Mr. Stilton demanded. "How do you explain all this?"

"Bad luck?" Tammy whispered, shrugging her shoulders.

"Perhaps, one of the legs buckled and gave out," I suggested, remembering the explanation I had used to appease the customers.

Glowering, and ready to fire the both of us, not to

mention the fact that I was still on shallow ground because of what the ghost of the little person had done, Mr. Stilton stomped over to the set of crumpled shelves that Tammy stood next to and investigated its support legs. His glower turned to intrigue before settling into a stern expression.

"It appears that there is a weakening here," he muttered to himself.

I was right. I had just guessed as a way to help Tammy out, but it turned out that I had been correct. I walked over to him and bent down, examining the legs and noticed one that had bent some, indicating that it was on the verge of giving out anyway.

"Get this stuff cleaned up," Mr. Stilton said to us. "I'll make some calls to get these shelves carted out and some new ones delivered, hopefully by morning."

Both Tammy and I rushed to the backroom and grabbed some empty boxes that a few deliveries had come in and used them to clean up what we could of the strewn merchandise. Some had to be tossed. To make it easier to dispose of the broken candles and shattered ceramic holders, I went out to the alley and brought in one of the garbage bins. Tammy remained in a quiet mood the rest of the day. Remembering her excitement about overhearing something, I decided to ask her about it. Maybe it would brighten her up. If anything, it would at least break this unsettling silence, broken only by Mr. Stilton's voice from his back office.

"So, tell me about this thing you overheard," I said to her.

Her eyes brightened. "So, you are interested?"

"Yes," I replied.

She scooted closer to me as though she was afraid of someone overhearing her. "Okay, so, I was standing there trying to get to you guys when a couple of officers started talking. They thought no one could hear them, but my ears can detect a mouse sniffing around in a crowded gym during a basketball game."

I bit my tongue to kept from laughing at such a notion. Tammy's self-praise would have made Jackie roll her eyes, but I did want to know what she might have overheard.

"I overheard them mention something about a set of tracks. Muddy tracks that they found within the tented area and they decided to search the culvert that is nearby."

"Muddy tracks?"

"Uh-huh!"

My mind mused over that puzzle for a moment. Yesterday had been sunny and…

"It wasn't raining," Tammy blurted out.

Despite her faults and eagerness to be involved in things, Tammy might have been onto something.

"Do you," I asked her, "remember if the woman that died had been wearing a scarf?"

Tammy shook her head. "I wasn't paying a lot of attention to the people on the stage."

That didn't surprise me.

"Mel?"

A culvert? I didn't know much about the layout of the city, but I'm sure I could find a map of the underground sewer system at the library. They had to have records of all building projects, maps, or blueprints. It was worth a try.

"Mel?"

I looked at Tammy and the perplexed look on her face, realizing that I had lost myself to my thoughts once again.

"You zoned out there for a second."

"Sorry," I said. "Let's finish this up so we can go home."

Tammy smiled and hummed a tune. My interest in what she had to say had cheered her up, making me glad since this time, the most recent disaster at the Candle Shoppe was not caused by anything she had done.

"You know," Tammy said, "maybe I shouldn't have tried to climb the shelves."

Okay. Scratch that last thought. "What?"

"Well, I wanted to make sure everything was organized perfectly so I thought I would start at the top shelf and climbed up."

"Why didn't you use the step stool?" I asked.

"We have a step stool?"

Chapter 3

I left work in the early afternoon. Once Tammy and I had finished cleaning up her mess, Mr. Stilton told us to leave.

"Hey, Mel, wait up!"

I stopped just as I tried to unlock my car, cringing when I recognized the voice. Tammy ran up, but she tripped over the edge of the sidewalk and bumped into the side of my car, muttering something that sounded like ow.

"Are you alright?" I asked her.

"Fine." She brushed a clump of hair that had draped itself over her stumpy nose and struggled with her frizzy mane in an effort to contain it and keep it from falling over face.

An awkward silence ensued as I stood there, my key ready to open the car door, waiting for Tammy to explain what she was doing here.

"Oh," said Tammy, looking around and noticing my growing impatience, "you are probably wondering what it is I want."

I nodded.

"I'm coming with you!"

"Uh… I have plans," I said.

Tammy pouted.

"Greg and I were planning on going out."

"Oh." Tammy's disappointment came through crystal clear.

"I'll see you tomorrow." I unlocked my car, got in, and started the engine, waving to Tammy as I left in an effort to be polite. She was a nice girl, but a lot to handle. Her exuberant personality made her a hard pill to swallow and she had a habit of causing a few disasters with her "brilliant" ideas. I think the only reason why Mr. Stilton didn't fire her was because one time I felt sorry for Tammy after one of her incidents and asked Rachel to help her get her job back. My boss hasn't been the same since.

I started back for the apartment, but what Tammy had said about the culvert and what she had overheard kept entering my mind, bugging me until I gave in, turning off the road that headed home and taking the one that went past the library. Once I arrived there, I parked in some shade, the only shade I could find, disappointing another patron who had coveted that spot, and went inside, reveling in the blast of cold air that struck me. I walked up to the front desk.

"May I help you?" asked an elderly lady, her hair pulled in a tight bun and a pair of reading glasses resting on the tip of her pointy nose, who looked like she should have been retired, but I shoved my personal thoughts aside.

"Yes," I replied. "I was wondering if you had any maps of the city."

"We do. Are you looking for any one in particular?"

"Blueprints mostly."

The woman walked out from behind the desk and I thought that her ankle length skirt looked a little dated, but passed it off as something unimportant since fashions tend to come and go and I was never one to pay much attention to it.

"I know," she said when she noticed me staring, "I haven't had a chance to do some washing."

I just smiled, hoping that she wasn't offended.

"We keep our maps of the city downstairs in the archives department," continued the woman, heading for the stairs, her low-heel pumps making soft clicks on the industrial carpeted floor.

I followed after her, allowing her to lead me. We trooped down the stairwell, her quick movements surprising me, and took the first door on the right once we reached the bottom. Solid wood and wide shelves four inches thick lined the walls, each overflowing with odd-sized volumes of books that looked like they weighed several pounds. A set of filing cabinets stood in the center of the room, surrounded by long tables meant for holding huge books or maps.

"This is where most of our old maps and blueprints for the city are," said the librarian. "We have some that date back to 1792, but you need special permission to view those and they are kept locked up in that climate controlled room over there"—she pointed to a solid steel door that had a huge sign that read "Authorized Personnel Only" on it—"but we are in the process of digitizing them so that the general public can view them."

"Now, over here"—she walked over to a set of shelves on our left that had a layer of dust on them an inch thick—"are some maps that date back to the 1800s and early 1900s. They are copies. We don't let people handle the originals." She reached for a leather-bound book that had the fold out maps in them and blew the dust off it, filling the air with the suffocating substance as I coughed and gagged.

"I'm sorry, dear," she apologized and I wondered why the dust didn't affect her, but was more interested in the maps. "And here"—she reached for another leather volume—"has the more recent maps of the city from 1950 on up to the present." She blew the dust from the top of the book.

"I'm guessing that not many people use these," I muttered.

The woman chuckled a little. "Is there anything specific you are looking for?"

"I just wanted to see if there was a culvert or tunnel that led underneath the park."

"I haven't heard of anything like that, but I think you will find that this will help you." She handed me the book she had been holding which contained the maps created within the last 70 years. "I'll leave you alone to do your research. Just lock up when you're done. And don't forget to turn the lights off. Saving energy, you know." She laughed at that last bit as she walked out the door, leaving me alone with shelves upon shelves of old books containing maps, bluprints, and old news articles.

I plopped the book on one of the long tables and

cringed at the sound it had made, wondering if I should have been more gentle. I glanced around to see if anyone else heard it, but I was alone in the archive room. The binding creaked as I opened the book and flipped through it, searching for something that would help me. The first map I looked at just showed the main roads of downtown. As I studied it, I noticed that some of the original buildings still stood, while others had been torn down and replaced, since the modern layout did not completely match this particular map.

I turned the pages to a new one and noticed a grayed-out area with the word "proposed" on it. As I looked closer, I realized that it was the park. I turned the page and found a blueprint for the park itself. The proposed perimeter of it was larger than what had been built in the end, but a small line extending from the park and through the city caught my attention. I grabbed a magnifying glass and looked closer. It was the sewer line. I followed the line on the map, taking note of the path it carved through the city, but noticed that it went underneath the park itself. A few dotted circles dotted the line itself, making me wonder if those were where the manholes were. I pulled out my phone and snapped a picture of it. Turning another few pages, I found a map that showed the completed park, but the marked sewer line looked a bit different. I turned back to the previous map before returning to the other one. The sewer line had been moved. I snapped a picture of this map just as my phone binged.

Where are you?

It was Jackie. I looked at the time, wondering why she had texted me since it was only three o'clock.

At the library, I texted her back.

Doing what?

Will explain when I get home. What's up?

Heard about Tammy's little mishap. 🌀

Will tell you about it later.

Hurry up!

👍

I put my phone back in my pocket, closed the book and placed it back in the gap on the shelf it had come from. Before leaving, I made sure everything had been put back the way it should be and turned off the lights like the librarian had asked me to. When I reached the main entrance of the library, I glanced at the circulation desk, but saw no sign of the elderly lady, but thought little of it. She might have been in the back or gone home.

I got in my car and drove off, heading for the park. I took the first available spot and hurried to the mowed lawn. According to the map, there should be a manhole near the east entrance, but I couldn't find it. A few people walked past and glanced in my direction, curious about why I wandered in circles, staring at the ground while holding my phone out. Not wanting to attract any more attention than I already received, I moved over to a lump of juniper bushes and pretended to be searching for a lost earring and that's where I found what I searched for. By the looks of it, it appeared that the bushes had been planted near the manhole, but as they grew, their branches covered it some, making it blend in with the landscape.

"You found it!"

I jumped, entangling myself in the juniper bushes and bumping my head against a prickly branch. As I freed myself from my spindly prison, I glared in the direction of who had spoken, startling me to the point that my heart skipped three beats, and found Tammy standing there with a crowbar.

"Tammy! What are you doing here?" I asked her through gritted teeth.

"I followed you," she replied. "You spent an awfully long time at the library."

"And the crowbar?"

She handed it out to me. "I thought you would need it."

I took the crowbar, still rubbing my head from where I had hit the branch. As Tammy watched, hovering over my shoulder the way a mosquito does while trying to find the right place to strike, I slid the crowbar into one of the holes in the manhole cover and heaved. The metal plated moved an inch before snapping back into place.

"A little help, please," I said to Tammy.

"Oh," she said and jumped by my side, grasping the crowbar.

Together, we yanked and struggled to pull it loose, but it was stuck tight with years of grime and buildup sealing it into place. When was the last time this thing had been opened? It popped free. We both landed on our behinds as the manhole cover flew out of its hole, landing on the ground, leaving us still holding onto the crowbar. I gave the crowbar back to Tammy.

Droplets of water dripped onto the ground, falling from the rim of the hole I now leaned over, looking down into a dark, dank, and murky tunnel. A ladder rested to the side of it, screwed into a concrete wall; its rusted, wet surface reflected the tiny amount of sunlight that shone through the hole. I rolled onto my stomach and threw my legs over the edge, finding the ladder with my feet and easing myself down until I gripped it with my hands.

"Where are you going?" asked Tammy.

"Down there," I replied.

She glanced over my shoulder, her nose scrunching up in disgust as she looked at the brown water beneath me. "It looks a little dirty down there."

"It's a sewer," I said, climbing lower and lower, trying not to cough from my nose's feeble attempts to not breathe in the putrid stench that surrounded me. My hands slipped a little when gripping the clammy rungs of the metal ladder and I had to hang onto them tighter and tighter to keep from losing my hold on it. Once I reached the last step, I jumped back, splashing in the brown water around me, spraying my legs.

I looked around the dim tunnel I stood in, wishing I had a flashlight and cursed myself for forgetting it. Something poked out of my back pocket. My phone. I grabbed it and used its flashlight function to try and shed some light on my surroundings. I waded through the water, wishing that it wasn't as deep as it was as it came halfway up my calves, vowing to throw my current pair of shoes away. Water flowed around my legs, carrying with it discarded wrappers, paper cups, and a few other things that made it down here from people who just tossed aside their trash instead of putting it in a waste bin, and there are several scattered throughout the city.

The powerful sound of water striking the bottom of a conduit caught my attention and I moved closer to a grate, doing my best to look down it without getting my head caught. The drop was too far down and I knew that no one had gone down there. I walked further down the tunnel, my feet splashing with each step I took, while I waved the weak light from my phone around me.

"Mel! Wait up!"

I stopped as Tammy navigated her way down the ladder, her feet stomping on each one, making so much noise that I was certain someone would hear us down here. She jumped off the bottom rung like I had, splashing in the water with her arms extended as though she were a gymnast ending her performance in the Olympics. I shook my head and turned away, stopping the moment I heard her shriek and whirled back around.

"What is it?" I asked, worried that something might have happened to her.

Tammy stood against the side of the tunnel, pressing herself against it as she pointed a shaking finger at a small, grayish-brown mound that seemed to be moving. I focused my beam of light on it.

"It's just a rat," I said.

Tammy sidestepped away from it, hugging the wall as she inched her way towards me never peeling her eyes away from the furry creature. "I don't like rats," she said.

Neither did I, but I wasn't about to tell her that. "Let's go," I said to her, urging her to move onward before the rodent could summon reinforcements.

We headed further in, rounding a corner, passing under

a few open drains, covered with metal grates, that allowed some light in, but not much. I kept my phone's flashlight focused ahead of us. A plop sounded behind us and Tammy jumped a little, probably thinking that the rat followed us.

"It's probably nothing," I reassured her.

Tammy nodded her head, looking around as we pushed our way through the murky tunnel, not noticing the stench as our noses had become accustomed to it.

I stopped.

"What is it?" Tammy asked.

I pointed ahead of me. A huge, tangled mass of vines and thorns protruded from the tunnel wall, closing off our pathway, except for a small opening that was just big enough for a child to squeeze through. I waved my light around and noticed cracks stretching up the concrete sides to the ceiling, stretching out in a lightning pattern. No wonder a plant sprung up here. It looked as though the city hadn't been down here in a while to do any repairs.

"What do we do now?" asked Tammy.

"We go through," I replied.

"It doesn't look like we'll fit."

Though she had a point, I did not want to turn back. I wanted to know where this thing led. "It's either that, or we go back to where the rats are."

Tammy pushed her way past me, flinging herself into the small space left open by the bramble, squeezing and shoving her way through amidst a torrent of cracks and snaps. Okay, that was fast.

"Come on!" Tammy urged me, no doubt frightened

that I might get attacked by a nefarious rodent. I didn't have the heart to tell her that there were probably more on the other side.

Hanging onto my only source of light, I turned and walked sideways through the slender opening, brushing my way past sharp thorns that scraped my skin and snagged at my jeans. A series of cracks resounded in the air, echoing off the curved walls of the sewer. Something caught my leg. I pulled, but it refused to let go. I tugged even more. Still no luck. Using my light to see what I had gotten caught on, I noticed that a vine had wrapped itself around my shin and the more I struggled, the more it tightened its hold.

A bit of orange caught my attention. Looking more closely, I saw a piece of sunset orange cloth hanging from a branch near when my leg had gotten caught. I reached for it and pulled it loose, holding it in my phone's light. The delicate tulle material waved as it dangled from my hand. Isn't this the sort of material that goes to a dress? Not knowing much about fashion, I knew I would need Jackie's help for this. She would know. She knew everything about clothes and what to wear for which occasion.

"Mel?"

"I'm stuck," I said, pocketing the piece of tulle material.

"Give me your hand."

I reached out for her and she grabbed my arm, yanking on it.

"Careful!" I yelled, afraid that she might pull my arm out of its socket.

"Sorry," Tammy whispered.

She pulled again, while I twisted and shook my leg in an effort to free myself from the bramble that seemed intent on holding me captive. With each passing second, I leaned further and further to the side. Tammy gave one more final yank. My shin ripped free of the vine and I fell into the murky water. As I hauled myself to my feet, shaking my arms in a pathetic attempt to dry them, Tammy screamed. She jumped around in the water, kicking at something that crawled along a ledge in an attempt to scurry away.

"Tammy, what—"

Before I had a chance to finish my question, one of Tammy's flailing arms smacked me in the face and I crashed back into the sewer water, taking another plunge in the city's nastiness.

"I think I got it," Tammy said through gasps as I sat up, coughing and spitting out tainted water, hoping I don't get sick from all of this. She paused and tilted her head to the side, giving me an odd glance. "This is no place to take a bath."

I could have killed her. Did it look like I'm taking a bath? "You punched me," I spat at her, trying to keep my voice under control, but its tightness came through regardless.

Tammy placed her hands over her mouth. "Oh—I'm sorry!"

"It's okay…"

"Here. Let me help you up."

"I think I've had enough help for now." I stood up on my own, wary of letting Tammy help me for a second time today in the same tunnel and checked my pocket to make sure that my only clue had not fallen out and gotten lost, which would be just my luck.

"What's that?" Tammy asked, noticing the sunset orange material for the first time.

"I found it over there."

She snatched it from me. I was about to scold her, but stopped when she spoke. "It looks like it belongs to an evening gown."

"Huh?" I said, confused.

"Yeah," replied Tammy. "This is tulle or gossamer, but I think it is tulle. It feels and looks more like it, even though the mud on it makes it a bit difficult to tell. I'd say it was the outer lining, or the outer shell of a formal dress. See this little bit of embroidery here? Definitely too fancy to belong to a piece of everyday clothing."

I gaped at her. Since when did she know so much about clothing? Her sense of fashion had always left so much to be desired. Remember the cockroach earrings? That was something I would never forget.

"What?" Tammy looked at me with wide, innocent eyes.

"I... uh... didn't realize you knew so much about clothing," I said, taking the piece of cloth back.

"I do make my own clothes," she huffed.

I bit my tongue to keep myself of saying something I would regret.

"Hey, do you think one of the pageant ladies came down here?" Tammy asked all excited.

"I don't know," I replied. "Right now, I am more interested in getting out of here."

I took the lead again, and raised my phone to shine its light so that we could see where we were going when it shut off. I tried to turn my phone back on, but all I received in return was a black screen. Great. My battery was dead. "Did you bring your phone?" I asked Tammy.

"Oh, yeah, it's right here." She pulled her phone from her pocket and held it out to me when it fell from her outstretched hand and into the disgusting water we stood in. That singular plop echoed around us, mocking us. I glared at her and if I had been wearing reading glasses, I'm sure my gaze would have gone over their rim.

"Oops?" said Tammy with an unsure grin. She reached down, plunging her hand into the water and waved it around as she searched for her phone. When she found it, she jumped back up and smacked me right in the chin. "Sorry!"

"Does it work?" I asked through gritted teeth, rubbing my sore chin.

"No," Tammy replied in a disheartened tone.

"Come on," I said.

I worked my way through the culvert, following the wall and using it to guide us, glancing behind me every so often to make sure Tammy remained behind me, hoping that we would find another manhole soon. There had to be one nearby. Our feet splashed and swooshed in the water as we waded through the sewer unsure of where we were going. The thought that we were nowhere near the next manhole entered my mind and I dreaded the probability of having to turn around and crawl through that mess of thorns. If someone came through here, they had a long distance to go, and the plausibility of someone using the sewer as a getaway seemed less and less likely. But where did that piece of tulle come from? Who would be down here wearing something like that?

A ray of light shown up ahead. I hurried, dragging Tammy behind me. I heard her call my name as I ran through the sewer, my feet kicking up water with each step, splashing more on my already dirtied clothes. That light had to be coming from somewhere and I wanted to know where.

"Mel!"

I stopped.

"Can't you slow down?"

I looked up, dancing around as I searched for our exit and found it.

"Mel?"

I pointed above me. Tammy followed my finger and smiled. Without warning, she jumped up, flailing her arms and screeching with joy. Upon landing, her knee buckled and she toppled over, plowing into me and, together, we both crashed into the murky, foul water.

What is this? The fourth time I've had a bath in this filth?

I sat up, coughing and spitting out the mucky liquid, doing my best not to swallow it, vowing to take an entire bottle of Vitamin C when I got home.

"You know," said Tammy, smacking her lips, "it doesn't taste half bad."

My stomach churned and threatened to expel its contents. "You also thought that a morgue was a good place to take a nap."

"It is. It's so peaceful there."

A little too peaceful. I stood up and walked over to where the manhole was and climbed the ladder. My hands clung to the metal and I paused, running my fingers down it, remarking at how clean it seemed to be, considering where it's located—no buildup of grime, dust, or cobwebs. I reached the manhole cover and pushed against it. It lifted with ease. Odd. The one we had gone through to enter the tunnel had taken both Tammy and me to move it.

I heard Tammy start up the ladder.

"Tammy, stay down there."

"What?"

I turned as best I could to face her. "Think about it. If someone did come down here yesterday, I don't think they used the hole we did to leave. It took the both of us to open it. Do you really think one person did?"

Tammy stepped off the ladder and back into the sewage below. "Just don't take too long."

"I won't," I promised and I crawled through the opening and onto soft green grass.

Pulling myself to my knees, I looked around, noticing the crime scene tape nearby, marking off the area where Melanie Sanders had died. A few people strolled by, giving me curious glances, but continued on without bothering to speak to me; not that I blamed them, since I must have looked and smelled terrible. I hurried over to the tents that had been left, ducking under the yellow tape and dashing through the opening flap of the first one I came to.

A few foldable chairs and tables were inside, forming a line with vanities at each table for the contestants to have plenty of light to put on their makeup. I stepped to the side and walked into a rolling cart that had just two dresses left hanging on it. One glance at them told me that they were not going to be of any interest to me. Neither of them matched the color of the cloth I had found in the sewer. Looking at the makeshift vanities, I decided to rifle through a few of the items still left, finding only lipstick, eyeliner, and some makeup brushes with powder residue on them.

Disappointed, I left that tent and hurried over to another one. It had the same setup, except most of the chairs and tables had been folded and stacked, waiting to be loaded onto a truck. Once again, my search ended in disappointment.

"Hey!"

I whirled around.

"What are you doing in here?" A woman with a clipboard had walked in on me and she looked anything, but pleased, to see me.

"I... I..."

"Who are you?" she demanded.

"No one," I replied.

"You're not supposed to be in here. I'm calling the cops."

That was the last thing I wanted. I did not need Detective Shorts finding out that I had come here. He would not be pleased.

Just then, the beeping of a truck backing up surrounded us and the woman put her phone down, looking out the tent flap and her already annoyed demeanor turned to rage. "What the hell do they think they're doing?"

She ran out of the tent, yelling and screaming at the truck driver.

Seizing my chance, I ducked outside and ran, but tripped over something poking out of the ground and fell on the ground. I lifted myself up and looked around to find what had caused me to fall and noticed a stake in the ground, it's green color blending in with the grass. I spotted another stake as well and realized that there had been a tent here, but someone had taken it down. As I rattled my brains about yesterday's event, I remembered that there had been three tents. A drop of water caught my attention. I turned my head and could not believe what I saw: a rectangular hole in the ground just big enough for someone of average size to squeeze through. I rushed over to it. As I leaned close, I heard the water below. I pulled at the grate covering the sewer and a screw dropped out of the top right corner. A few more tugs told me that the entire grate was loose and the screws had only been placed back in, not secured.

"I saw her over here," came the familiar irate voice.

I needed to leave. Knowing that I would never make it to back to the manhole I had come out of, nor could I run away in time without being spotted, I chose my only other option: the sewer next to me. I yanked at the grate and it pulled free with ease, surprising me a little and as my mind started to wonder why this was so, the woman's angry voice drawing closer forced me to forget my curiosity. I went in feet first and eased myself through the slender opening, wiggling some to squeeze my butt through. My dangling feet found nothing but air and I had to hold myself with one hand while I used the other to put the grate back in place.

"I'm telling you she was over here."

Once I had the grate over the opening—it wasn't perfect and someone would notice it sooner or later—I pushed myself backward and hoped that the drop wasn't too far. I splashed in the water below and my legs crumpled beneath me, causing me to fall on my behind, taking another bath in the filthy liquid. I could not wait for the chance to take a shower. It would probably take a week to get this stench out of my hair.

I needed to find Tammy. I forced myself to my feet and looked around, wondering which way I should go, when a hushed voice calling my name, followed by two footsteps, answered my question. I tiptoed down the tunnel, doing my best not to make too much noise, following the flowing water as I navigated my way through. Turning a corner, I noticed Tammy's back facing me as she waited for me to return.

"Tammy," I whispered.

She shrieked and jumped.

"Tammy, it's just me," I said, trying to calm her.

"Mel… how… you were…"

"I found another way in."

"Where?" Tammy's confusion turned to intrigue.

"Down that way."

She started off in the direction I pointed and I snatched her arm. "But we can't go that way now."

"Why?"

"There's people up there and none of them liked me being there. We need to leave and we're going to have to go back the way we came."

Tammy stared down the long culvert as her mouth turned into a frown.

"I'll protect you from any rats we find," I coaxed.

"Promise?" she asked, reminding me of a toddler

when they don't want to do something and you make a promise just to get them to go along.

"Promise," I replied, not sure how I would protect her from any rodent we might find, but my desire to leave outweighed my fears.

Tammy nodded and took off down the sewer with me right behind her, her wish to leave matching my own sentiments.

Chapter  4

I placed my hand on the knob of the door to my apartment and turned it, but before I could open the door, it flung out of my hand and Jackie stood there, filling the doorway. "So, where have you been? What's this big—what is that smell!"

"May I come in, please?" I asked, feeling exhausted and not liking the way Jackie held her nose.

"Where did you go?"

"Jackie, I'd really like to…"

"Fine, but you're not tracking that stuff in here."

"But—"

"Just wait a minute," she said, running to the pantry, "and take off your shoes!"

I slipped off my shoes, not bothering to untie them.

When I looked up, a trash bag had been placed on the floor right in front of me. I examined the rest of the apartment and couldn't believe what Jackie had done, nor how fast she had managed it while I took my shoes off. A line of trash bags stretched from the front door to the bathroom, forming a path for me to walk on so that nothing would get tracked on the carpet.

"There," she said, pointing to her handiwork. "Come on. Chop! Chop! To the showers!"

"I stepped onto the first garbage bag and it crinkled under my toes."

"Wait!"

"What?"

"Perhaps you should take your clothes off there," Jackie suggested.

"I'm not stripping naked in the hallway!"

"No, you're right." Jackie waved me inside.

"Stripping naked? That sounds like—OH!"

I turned and found Greg standing behind me, having just gotten home and holding his nose.

"What happened?" he asked.

"I really just want to shower," I said.

Greg stared at me, debating whether he should push for the story of how I came to smell as though I had been buried in manure, or waiting until I had a chance to scrub every last ounce of the filth off me. He chose the latter. "I got some errands to run anyway."

"Yeah, you go"—Jackie pointed at Greg before turning to me—"And you, get in the shower."

Yes, ma'am. I didn't say that out loud, though. Instead,

I followed the garbage bags to the bathroom, making certain to stay on Jackie's impenetrable plastic path. Once in the bathroom, I turned and faced her.

"How much detergent do you think it will take to get your clothes clean?" she asked me.

"Just hand me a bag," I told her, resigning myself to the fact that the clothes on my body were ruined and too far gone to be saved. I didn't want to deal with it.

"An even better idea." She snatched the bag closest to her from the floor, handing to me and I took it, closing the door.

"Do you mind if I use your fruity shampoo?" I asked her through the door.

"Use the whole bottle! And the coconut body wash," she called through the door.

I smiled at her insistence and stripped off my clothes, stuffing them in the sack and tying it shut before handing it to Jackie who stood just outside the door. She snatched it from me, having gotten the rubber gloves from the kitchen to protect her hands. I pulled back the shower curtain and sighed. This was going to take a while.

After spending what felt like hours scrubbing, washing, rescrubbing, and rewashing to the point where my skin and scalp felt like they had both been scoured to the point of having nothing left to scrub, I turned off the water and grabbed my towel. A quick glance in the mirror made me want to shriek as I toweled off. My hair looked worse than usual, all knotted and tangled to the point where a rat could have had a nest in it. My red skin screamed for lotion and I snatched some of Jackie's special body moisturizer. I'd buy her a new bottle later.

Once I had finished beautifying myself as best I could, or at least making it so my skin felt a little less itchy, I wrapped my towel around me and tip-toed across the hall to my room.

My computer's screen blinked at me through the thin material of the shirt I pulled over my head and I had a thought. Melanie Sanders claimed to be from an old Vermont family: the Beaumonts; but I knew nothing about them. I wondered if I would be able to learn any-thing about them online. I pulled up a web browser and typed in their name.

A few results just brought up urban legends about a family fortune that went missing. One site said it went missing during the Civil War, while another claimed that it had been given to the Nazis during World War II. I closed those sites and ignored them. Neither told me what I wanted to know and I had little interest in urban legends.

Old Families of the United States, said one search result.

I clicked on it, opening a new tab within my browser. A huge list of each state and the "old" families that had set-tled them popped up. Luckily for me, there was an alphabet bar at the top, allowing me to click on the letter I needed. I scrolled my mouse over the V and clicked it, forcing the page to scroll downward, bringing me to the section where Vermont was listed. A bunch of names appeared, but after quick scan, I found what I wanted: the name Beaumont.

I clicked the link and another page popped up.

The Beaumonts are one of the oldest families within the state of Vermont, tracing their genealogy to the aristocracy of France. Louvel Beaumont, the son of Pépin Dubois, a member of the French court, had been disowned by his father and chose to seek redemption in the New World, where he abandoned his father's surname and took his mother's maiden name instead. He and his wife made the arduous voyage and settled in what would later be called Vermont in 1715.

The text ended there with a link for me to click, so that I could become a member and gain access to the rest of the Beaumont's genealogy. I closed the page. I hated it when a promising website suddenly asked you for more money just to access the coveted information they claimed to hold. Scrolling down my list of search results I found another that seemed interesting and opened it up.

The Beaumont Conspiracy!

The Beaumont family claims to be have settled in the 1700s, but they really settled in 1918 in an effort to escape the influenza epidemic of Europe. Don't believe their incessant lie about a family fortune. Their real fortune lies within their connection to aliens and the UFO conspiracy created by the men in black, headed by Will Smith.

Wait? What?
I scrolled to the bottom of the page where the author's biography was and realized that this was nothing more

than a satirical website, meant to give people a laugh. Several of the comments at the bottom read, "LOL!", "Ha-Ha", or had smiley face emojis. I closed the page.

Frustrated that I was not getting anywhere, I tried another search and typed in "Melanie Sanders Beaumont connection" into the search bar. Over a thousand results showed up and I scrolled through the page, ignoring the ones that were obvious opinion pieces or bloggers just wanting to get in on the woman's death. One result stuck out: *Was Melanie Sanders one of the Beaumonts?* I clicked on it.

If any of you know anything about the state of Vermont, you probably already know that it was never one of the 13 original colonies. A part of the territory had been given to the Duke of York by King Charles II, and Vermont suffered from constant territorial disputes with New York as a result. Settled by both the French and the British, Vermont declared its own independence in 1777, and like California and Texas, became its own republic, until 1791 when it became the first state to be admitted to the union, thus becoming the 14th state.

Why this history lesson, you ask? It's simple. As mentioned earlier, both the French and British settled in Vermont and one such person to do so was Louvel Beaumont, supposed ancestor of the late Melanie Sanders.

Miss Sanders, a rising star in the various local beauty

pageants, had made repeated claims that she was a descendent of the Beaumont family. How true are her claims? Let's investigate, shall we?

Louvel Beaumont and his wife sailed across the Atlantic and reached Vermont territory in 1715 where they settled on a small plot of land that they had purchased. They had settled on what could have been called the frontier in those days and they suffered from a few Indian attacks and it did not help that there were constant disputes between the British and the French themselves. Despite the harsh life of the New World, he managed to make a fruitful living as a fur trader and his wife Marie bore him three sons, one of whom made it to adulthood. Their son married a British girl, whose family had immigrated from England a few years prior to their marriage, and had two sons: Samuel and Jean.

During the French and Indian War, both Samuel and Jean joined the fight, but on opposing sides. Samuel fought for the British, while Jean joined the French, but died two years into the war. When the war had ended, Samuel returned home and took over the family estate. He married the daughter of a prominent businessman, expanding his own ventures and profits. They had three children: two sons and one daughter. Only their daughter, Jocelyn, survived childhood.

Their first-born son died in infancy and their second son, Abel, died at the age of 12 from a small smallpox outbreak while visiting relatives in Massachusetts.

Jocelyn married a man named George Hamilton and had six sons. Four of her sons died during the War of 1812. Her remaining two, John and Ramond, survived, but their stories are equally tragic. John's wife died during childbirth and he succumbed to depression, taking his own life in 1817. Ramond married, but he and his wife never had any children. He died at the age of 46, just before the start of the Civil War.

And this is where the story of the Beaumonts ends. Is Melanie Sanders one of their descendants? The only way for that to be a possibility is if someone within the family had illegitimate children from an illicit affair, but there is no definitive proof that such a thing happened. It is up to you to decide if Miss Sanders lied, for reasons that are her own, or told the truth and really is a lost heir.

Melanie Sanders lied?

I guessed that it was possible that she had, but the question remained, why would she do such a thing? If her ruse had been discovered, she could have lost everything. Though, these days, most people did not care about family trees and whether someone came from some family that could trace their lineage back several generations, but that didn't answer the question of why she made her claim in the first place. Unless she was, as the author of the article suggested, the descendant of an illegitimate child, fathered by one of the Beaumont males. Such a thing is not unusual. I needed to contact the author of the article. I hit the page down button and found the author's name and picture, pausing to stare at it for several moments. He looked familiar. Several links were there as well and I clicked on one, which took me to a sales page for one of his books and that's when it clicked: he was at the park yesterday. I had glanced through one of his books about the history of Vermont. I wondered if he was local or lived elsewhere and only came here for the event in the park.

A quick glance at his biography page didn't tell me much. It gave the typical paragraph about his credentials and a listing of his books, but—Oh! An email address.

My phone buzzed and I checked the latest text message to arrive on it, surprised that it still worked after having been drenched a couple of times today. The message was from Mr. Stilton, informing me that the new shelves would be put up tonight and I was to open in the morning and work as usual, though, he would take the day off, which meant I would have to lock up at the end of the day.

"Hey, Mel, are you okay in there?" Jackie called through the door.

"I'm fine," I replied and clicked on the email address which brought up my own email service and a ready to compose message. Before Jackie had a chance to become more worried about my seclusion, I typed up a simple message, expressing my interest in the Beaumonts and if we could meet.

"Mel?"

I jumped out of my chair with some excitement and ripped my door open. "She may not be a Beaumont!"

"What?" Jackie stared at me with a confused look on her face.

"I've been doing some reading on the Beaumont family," I replied.

"Is that why you have been locked in here for the past two hours?"

I checked my clock. Two hours? I hadn't even noticed the time pass.

"Do you want to tell me what you were doing this afternoon and why you came home smelling like you had been crawling around in a sewer?"

"Probably because I had been."

Jackie put her hands on her hips.

I took a deep breath and started from the beginning. I had promised to tell Jackie everything when I got home and now was the time to come clean. "Tammy had mentioned that she had overheard the police talking about how some tracks led to a culvert. According to her, they had planned on investigating the sewers that run underneath the park."

"And you believed her?" asked Jackie.

I shrugged my shoulders, knowing what she thought, but it turned out that Tammy had been right.

"Of course, you did," said Jackie.

"I found something," I said.

Jackie's eyes lit up. "You did?"

"I found a piece of cloth, but"—my tone changed when Jackie's face turned into a doubtful scowl—"it was made from some sort of fancy material—tulle I think. Not the sort of everyday cloth you would expect to find. And I think it matched an outfit one of the contestants had been wearing."

The doubtful expression on Jackie's face turned into one of curiosity. "Where is it?" she asked.

"It was in my pocket when I got home," I said.

"Your pocket?"

"I think I took it out and placed it on the table by the door, but…"

"The table?" Jackie's voice had a worried edge to it.

"Yeah. Let me go get it."

"By the door?"

I faced Jackie. "I believe so. Why?"

Jackie wrung her hands together in that nervous pose of hers, the one she gets when she is afraid that she might have done something wrong. "Now, don't get mad—"

"Mad?"

"—but I think I might have seen what you're talking about."

"And?" I asked, the pit in my stomach filling with dread.

"Well, you had handed me your clothes and told me to throw them out and, then, I saw this grungy piece of orange cloth hanging off the table by the door and just assumed that it was part of the whole kit and caboodle that you wanted thrown away."

"Where is it?"

As though in answer to my question, the beeping sound of a dump truck backing up came through the window, laughing at me.

"The dumpster," said Jackie.

I ran to the window and looked outside, my heart sinking as I watched the dump truck lift up the dumpster and drop all the contents within it. "I need that cloth."

"But—"

"It was evidence!"

I ran out the door and tore down the hallway, flinging the door to the stairwell open and charged down the stairs to the parking area. The sound of the dumpster being dropped on the ground echoed around me. I never paused in my haste to get out there and ran, barefoot, across the pavement to the fenced in area where the dumpsters were kept. By the time I reached it, the garbage truck had already pulled away. I stared after it, breathing hard, but kept my gaze fixed on the license plate, repeating the number to myself until I had it memorized, hoping that I would be able to do something to rectify this entire situation.

"Mel!" Jackie ran up to me.

"Look around. Maybe it fell out."

I searched around the dumpsters, jumping up on the side and peering over the edge, finding nothing but empty, odorous space below. My hopes dashed, I slumped against the side of one of the dumpsters, blowing a piece of hair out of my face.

"Mel, I'm sorry," apologized Jackie.

"It's not your fault," I said. "I should have said something when I first came home.

Just then, Greg's car pulled into the parking lot. He must have seen us, because he drove right up to us instead of parking in his usual spot. "Hey," he said, rolling down his window. "I thought you'd be dressed and ready to go."

"Go?" I said, confused.

"Dinner," he replied.

Oh my gosh! I forgot!

"What are you doing out here, anyway?" he asked.

"I lost something and now the garbage truck has it," I replied.

When a perplexed expression crossed Greg's face, Jackie answered his unspoken question. "This afternoon, Mel found something that could be a clue and I accidentally threw it away."

"Clue?" he asked.

"I don't think that woman's death yesterday was an accident," I said.

He nodded his head and stepped out of the car. "I'd been thinking about that. So, you found something?"

"I think so," I said, "but it's gone now." I glanced in the direction of the garbage truck.

"Too bad Tiny's not here," mumbled Jackie.

That's it! If anyone could help us, it was Tiny. "Do you have your phone?" I asked Greg.

He handed me his cell phone. "Who are you calling?"

"Tiny," I replied. "If anyone can hijack a garbage truck, it's him."

I dialed Tiny's number. He picked up on the first ring. "Tiny!"

"Hey, Mel. I was just thinking about you."

"How would you feel about borrowing something that belongs to the city?"

"Name it," said Tiny.

"It's a garbage truck. The number sixty-seven is on the side in orange lettering and the license plate number is six, nine, nine with the letters m, x, and z on it."

"Be at the old Lars Warehouse in an hour." He hung up.

I smiled as I handed Greg back his phone.

"Well?" both he and Jackie asked.

"He'll do it," I said.

That was the thing about Tiny. He never minded breaking the law for any of his friends. Stealing a garbage truck was right his alley.

Chapter 5

"Are you sure he said to meet him here?" Greg asked as we pulled up to the old warehouse Tiny had told us to meet him at and parked in front of the gigantic steel door.

"That's what he said," I replied, growing a little worried as I looked around the desolate area, wondering where everyone was.

"It looks a bit abandoned," said Greg.

"That's because it is," quipped Jackie from the back seat. "Maybe you should call Tiny and find out where he is."

I agreed and had been thinking the same thing. Just as I pulled out my phone and dialed his number, a horn blared, piercing my ears and making me cringe. I looked up and saw a garbage truck heading straight for us with an escort of motorcycles; their thunderous roars echoed around us, causing the glass in the few windows of the building to vibrate. Two of Tiny's men raced up to the double doors and jumped off their bikes, running for the entrance and pulled the doors open, allowing the garbage truck to park inside, while the rest of the bikers followed.

"We should do the same," I said.

Greg started up his car again and drove into the warehouse, parking near where the other bikes had been left just as the doors closed behind us. One by one, engines turned off and the deafening noise quieted to something more tolerable.

Tiny jumped out of the cab of the truck. "Well, here you are."

He stood there with his arms crossed and I knew he waited for me to give him an explanation of why I had him steal this garbage truck. Before giving him what he wanted, I circled the vehicle, checking the license plate number and the numerals on the side of the truck, making certain that it was the right one, and it seemed to be. "I am starting to think that the woman who died yesterday was actually murdered and there might be some evidence in this garbage truck."

"How would it end up here?" asked one of Tiny's men.

"I accidentally threw it away," said Jackie in a quiet voice, still embarrassed by the whole situation.

"Did you stick it in the same garbage bag that my clothes had been in?" I asked her.

"Yeah," replied Jackie. "It was a black garbage bag"—a few groans echoed around us since almost every garbage bag was black—"but it had a blue draw string."

That narrowed it down some. At least we could throw out the ones with a red draw string.

"You heard her!" Tiny shouted to his gang. "Get to it!"

Someone hopped into the cab and opened the rear of the garbage truck. It lifted up and out spilled all its contents, complete with the stench of rotted food, decaying rats, other decomposing organic matter masked in a swarm of flies that had gotten caught up in it all. Well, it looks as though I will be taking another shower tonight. I stepped up to the pile of refuse and grabbed a black bag with a red drawstring, tossing it aside and starting a pile of discards. The crunching of plastic and paper filled the giant warehouse as others walked into the makeshift landfill and sorted through the bags, following my lead of creating piles.

Hours passed as we sifted through the mess, our piles growing higher and higher, forming their own version of a house of cards, which I thought could topple at any moment. The discard pile remained the largest, but we had managed to form a good-sized mound of possibilities: black bags with blue drawstrings. As we worked, Tiny remained close to me, wanting answers and I told him about my excursion into the sewer under the park and what I had discovered under there. A mixture of intrigue and disappointment crossed his face, telling me that he had wished I had invited him along instead of Tammy, and it didn't matter that I had told him that Tammy had invited herself against my wishes.

Once we had gotten the main pile of garbage sorted out, the next step was to delve into the heap of possibilities. I made my way to it and started ripping open bags, pulling out the contents, knowing right away that the first few I had grabbed were not the ones I searched for, since none of my clothes were in them. Jackie tore through the bags as well, opening them with a fervor I had never witnessed before, causing me to be a little concerned about her.

"It's okay," I told her, trying to soothe her.

"I just feel bad," she said. "You went through all that trouble to get this in the first place and I discarded it like it was nothing."

"I can't blame you. I would have done the same."

"But what if it's the only thing that helps solve this woman's murder?"

"We'll find it."

I snatched another bag and opened it. Nothing. I tossed it aside. Greg handed me another bag, but I ended up with the same result. Some of Tiny's men grew restless and he put them to work, shoveling all of this crap back into the garbage truck. Besides, they had to get the darn thing back to the city dump before anyone noticed it was missing, or before the police figured out that we had it.

"I think I found it," said Greg, opening another bag.

Jackie grabbed it from him and ripped it open, pulling out my shirt and pants that I had worn this afternoon. "Is this it?" she asked, handing me a grungy piece of sunset orange material.

"Yes." I took the material and tried cleaning some of the grime off it, but it turned out to be a pointless endeavor. "Does anyone have anything I can use to clean this?" I asked.

Tiny handed me a beer can.

"Not that," I said. "I want to clean this."

"Don't you think it will wash away any chance of identifying it?" asked Greg.

"Maybe," I answered, "but considering how much we're handling it and where we just got it from, I don't think it will make a difference."

Someone tossed me a bottle of water. I opened it and poured it over the piece of cloth, washing away some of the dirt and slime, revealing a somewhat brighter shade of orange. Jackie took it from me when I had finished cleaning it as best I could. She ran it through her fingers, studying it, looking at the edges and feeling the quality of the material itself.

"It is definitely tulle," she said, speaking to herself more than to us, "but a more expensive kind. Your hunch that it belonged to a dress, a formal one, was good. I would say that it was probably part of the outer lining, the part that adds decorative flair to the gown."

"How can you tell?" asked Greg, staring at the sunset orange piece of material and voicing my own thoughts. I didn't know much about dresses as I rarely wore them.

"See this detailing here?" Jackie pointed at a portion of the cloth where there seemed to be some sort of embroidery, but it matched the color of the tulle itself that I never noticed it; though, when the light hit it just right, it did seem to shimmer a littler. "It adds a little extra pizazz to the dress."

"But who would be running around in the sewer with an outfit like that on?" asked Greg.

"Someone who was desperate," said Tiny.

"But wouldn't the police have noticed a woman wearing a nice dress that had been torn?" Greg asked.

"With everything going on," said Jackie, "not likely."

I pondered Greg's question a moment. As I thought about it, I remembered the number of tents that had been set up and how some of them were changing tents with roll about carts filled with outfits for the contestants to wear, and each contestant usually had their own wardrobe to avoid wearing the same attire as one of the others. "What if the person had a second dress. One exactly like the one this piece of material came from?"

"It's possible," said Jackie. "At these sorts of events, most of the contestants have multiple pieces of the same outfit. That means it is possible that the wearer of this dress had another just like it."

"Why, though?" asked Greg.

"Sometimes clothes get dirty or ruined, or they just start to look dull. Under stage lights, a person will sweat, so, they need another of the same outfit to change into so that they always look fresh and new when they are called back out on stage. But not every contestant will have doubles of their outfits made."

Makes sense. If a woman had spilt juice or water on her evening gown and she was supposed to be on stage within minutes wearing that outfit, she would need another just like it to wear on the stage, or risk losing the contest. "We need a way to investigate the other contestants, but I don't think they will talk to just anyone," I said.

Jackie got a look on her face. I had seen it before. It's the same expression she gets when she is thinking of doing something rash.

"We should go home," Greg said.

"Good idea." Tiny waved his hand and three of his guys opened the double doors while one of his men jumped into the cab of the truck, started the engine, and backed out of the warehouse. "They know where to take it."

My phone binged. I checked the new text message and frowned. "You better tell them to hurry"—I showed Tiny the message from Detective Shorts—"because the police already know that it's been stolen."

Greg ushered Jackie and me to his car.

"Thanks, Tiny," I said, patting his shoulder.

"Hey, anytime you want to bend the law, I'm your man."

I chuckled. "How is it you were able to use this place? It's been abandoned for that last couple of years."

"I know a guy, who knows a guy, who owes me."

I expected that answer. Tiny didn't always reveal how he was able to bend the law, as he called it, and manage to get away from it. "Is there anyone in this city who doesn't owe you a favor?"

"Nope."

Greg whistled at me and I knew we had to leave. Jackie had already gotten in the back seat. I hurried over and climbed into the passenger seat, clutching the piece of material that Tammy and I had found earlier.

"I think I'm going to have to borrow your fruity shampoo again," I said to Jackie.

"Only if I get to use it first," she replied with a grin as Greg pulled out of the warehouse and headed home. "By the way, I have some for you too," she said to him.

"Um… thanks," Greg replied.

Chapter 6

The next morning, I left my room, dressed, clean, and ready to get to work to open the store. I was a little surprised that Mr. Stilton trusted me to open the store again, considering that not long ago I had been close to getting fired, though that had a little something to do with a ghost causing me to get arrested. I walked through the hallway and to the kitchen, finding something that occurs on the rarest of occasions: a plate with eggs, bacon, and toast with jam, complete with a filled glass of orange juice.

"What's this?" I asked Jackie.

"Nothing," Jackie replied in a sing-song voice as she poured me a cup of coffee and pushed the half and half towards me.

"You cooked me breakfast."

"Yeah. So?" She put the coffee carafe back in the coffee maker.

"Aren't you eating?" I asked her.

"Oh, I already ate. Now dig in! You have a long day ahead of you and after yesterday, you have to be hungry."

I took a bite of my eggs and bacon while my stomach growled, reminding me how hungry I was. Jackie hummed to herself as she finished up a few remaining dishes and my suspicions about all this grew. "Jackie, what's going on?"

"Nothing," she said, her tone too innocent.

"Are we now dating?" I asked in a joking matter.

"What? No!"

"Well, what gives? The only time you ever make me breakfast is when you are up to something, or want something, or both."

"I don't want anything," insisted Jackie. "I just thought you might like a nice breakfast before going off to work and dealing with Tammy."

I took another mouthful of egg.

"Though, I could use your signature on this." Jackie shoved a consent form in front me.

"I knew it." I put my fork down.

"It's nothing."

I pulled the paper closer to me and started reading it.

"I just need your signature right there." She placed a pen on the line at the bottom, indicating where I should sign.

"Are you evicting me?" I asked.

"No! Besides, if I did, then your aunt would try to move in with me."

"Oh, she wouldn't do that."

"Yes, she would. She's already tweeted about it."

Aunt Ethel knows how to use social media? That could not be good. Jackie showed me a post by my aunt, proving her fears of my aunt moving in with her if I moved out to be valid.

When my Mellow is 👫 will move in with her friend to save 💵. Can't wait! 😏

Hmmmm. Not a good sign. And she tweets in emoji? How and when did she learn that? It appears that my crazy aunt is adapting to this new world of social media quite nicely, while I never use my account.

"See? After you're married, she plans to move in here!"

"So, what does that have to do with this?" I asked, picking up the form she wanted me to sign.

"You said yesterday that you needed a way to snoop around the pageant ladies and their belongings. There is another local pageant going on this week and it ends on Sunday. All of the contestants who were at the July Fourth one are going to be at this one. I know because I looked them all up. This is a consent form to participate in the local pageant, while stating that you understand that all outfits loaned to you are owned by the city."

"The city owns the dresses?"

"It's a community thing. Come on. Just sign." She held the pen out to me.

"Jackie, this is more your thing. I'm not pageant material. I hate dresses. And heels?"

"I know. It will take a little work to get you all ready, but—"

"There has to be another way. I'm not—oh my gosh! I'm going to be late!"

I snatched my wallet and phone and headed for the door, but Jackie stood there with the consent form and a pen. I gave her a "you've got to be kidding me" look and dodged around her, running down the hallway and stairwell and to my car.

I pulled up to the Candle Shoppe just in time to unlock the doors and clock in. I shoved my stuff in my locker and found a note stuck there asking me to make sure our warmers were highlighted for the day. Throwing the note away, I grabbed a box of wax warmers that needed to be put on a display shelf before opening time. The quiet allowed me to do some thinking about what had happened yesterday as I prepared to get everything ready, knowing that both Tammy and Jackie would be there soon.

As I brought the box of warmers out, I noticed that the new shelves had no inventory on them, not that I was surprised. I didn't expect Mr. Stilton to actually stock the shelves, knowing that he would leave it for me to do. Making quick work of the warmer display, I finished it up and ran to the back, snatching boxes and boxes of tealight and votive candles, before grabbing some of our fancy glass candle holders. For an hour, I worked on filling the empty shelves, doing my best to make them look organized and inviting, hoping that people would at least purchase a few things so that my hard work did not go to waste.

A knock sounded on the door. Tammy had arrived on time, wearing a pair of red, yellow, and pink pants underneath a coral blue lace miniskirt. Her white tank top looked a little underdressed when compared to the rest of her outfit. I opened the door to let her in and she burst inside in her usual exuberant manner.

"Morning, Mel! I had a great time yesterday. Sharing one of your adventures has really brightened up my life and let me know what I am missing."

"Which is?" I asked.

"Excitement!"

"Try skydiving."

"I don't like heights."

Pity.

Jackie arrived and I let her inside, leaving the door unlocked since we were supposed to be open by now. "Where's our ever-present boss?" she asked with a note of sarcasm.

"Gone for the day, remember?"

Mr. Stilton had decided to take the day off, leaving me in charge of opening and closing the store, which meant I was going to have a long shift, with only an hour in between for lunch. I didn't mind too much. Extra hours meant extra money. The only downside was that my entire day was spent at work.

Customers came in soon after the doors opened, which surprised me because we normally did not have so many sales this late in the summer season. The bulk of our business was around Christmastime. Tammy followed me wherever I went, staying close by my side and almost tripping me a few times, annoying me so much, that I gave her the task of dusting the shelves, hoping that it would keep her busy. The one time I had to do it, it took me all day because you have to pull everything off the self, wipe them, and put everything back on.

"Why?" she pouted when I handed her a dusting rag and some spray.

"Because it needs to be done" I replied, keeping the part about how she was driving me nuts to myself.

She moaned, but took the dusting rag and spray.

My phone chirped at me, informing me that I had a new email message. Even though phones were forbidden at work, that never stopped any of us from using ours from time to time and this might have been a reply to the message I had sent last night. I opened my email app and frowned. The recipient of my message last night had not responded. I took a closer look at the new message.

Congratulations, it read, *on entering the Miss Belle pageant. We look forward to working with you. Be at the Civic Center tonight at 7pm.*

What?

I marched straight up to Jackie with my phone in my hand, pulling her away from the front counter.

"What?" she asked, annoyed.

I showed her the email message.

A sheepish smile crossed her face and her cheeks turned red. "That got out a little quicker than I had thought it would."

"I never signed that form," I said, trying to keep my voice low.

"Technically…"

"Jackie?"

"I maybe… kind of… sort of… forged your signature."

"What!"

My outburst caused a few people to look in our direction. I smiled at them, feeling embarrassed, and pulled Jackie even further away from the front counter. "Why did you do it?" I asked her.

"You know this is the only way to get close to those girls and snoop around."

She had a point, but the last time I chose to pretend to be a performer, I almost got hurt and my acting skills are so terrible that I would never be able to pass for a performer of any kind. "Jackie, you know I'm not good at this sort of thing. The other contestants will single me out as a fake and fraud really quick."

"Exactly," replied Jackie, "which will allow me to get close to them. We'll bond over your ineptitude."

"A bit devious, don't you think?"

"But it will work. You're a terrible performer, but women like these pageant ladies love to talk trash about one another and you will make a great conversation opener."

"You're really not helping my ego," I said.

"You're still my best friend."

"You know, forging a signature is illegal," I hissed.

"So is stealing a garbage truck," Jackie whispered back.

Except, technically, we didn't steal it. Tiny did. I just gave him the idea which would make me an accessory—okay, okay, Jackie had a point.

"You're entering the beauty contest?" Tammy ran out from where she had been hiding, waving her can of dusting spray, and talking loud enough to alert everyone in the store to our secret conversation.

"Were you listening to us?" I asked.

"I was cleaning those shelves over there and I heard you say something about the pageant and entering and— can I join you guys? Please! Please! Please!"

"Tammy…"

"Oh, let me! Let me! Let me!"

"It might be a little too…" began Jackie, her hands on her hips.

"Actually," said a voice none of us recognized, "you can go down to the civic center and fill out a form right there. You just have to get it in before seven tonight."

An elderly lady with her hair in a bun walked up to us and the feeling of déjà vu struck me, but why was it I could never remember where I had seen her before? "You work at the library, don't you?" I asked.

"I volunteer there," she replied.

"Tammy, the shelves," I whispered to my overexcited coworker. Disappointment filled her face, but she stomped off and continued with the cleaning of the shelves.

I noticed someone standing by the register and glanced at Jackie, who understood my message and went over to help the customer.

"May I help you," I asked the woman, marveling at how our roles had reversed to where I am the one assisting her.

"Yes, I was wondering if you had any lavender, tea tree, and peppermint oils. Being a candle store, I thought that, perhaps, you all would have an aromatherapy section, but I can't seem to find it."

"We have a small one over here." I led her to the far back corner of the shop where our miniscule aromatherapy section was. Mr. Stilton planned to expand it one day, but most people go to a natural health store for essential oils and I asked the woman about that. "Some of our oils may not be suitable for rubbing onto bare skin," I said. "Are you sure you wouldn't rather go to the health food store down the street?"

"They didn't have what I was looking for."

"If you don't mind my asking," I began, "what do you need them for?"

"Well, I'm a little embarrassed. I've lived here for a long time and am well aware of the nuances of poison ivy. There's some that grows around my house, you see. I'm afraid I got some on me when pulling it out."

"Have you considered weed killer?" I asked, since most people would have just sprayed the unwanted plant with it.

"I hate the stuff and it's bad for the wildlife."

"We have some oils over here"—I showed her the aromatherapy section and noticed Tammy watching every move I made, while her hand wiped the shelves in a robotic manner—"but you are going to want to double check and make sure that these oils can be applied to the skin."

"I'm not worried about that."

Really? She should be. It could make the poison ivy rashes worse. "I'll leave you to get what you need and might I suggest you wear long sleeves next time."

"I had," replied the woman, stopping me.

"Then, how…"

"Funny thing, really," the woman continued talking, not caring if I had other things to attend to, and being a customer, I decided it was best to humor her so that she would hopefully purchase a few of our oils. "I had worn a shirt with long sleeves and pants—very unladylike, I know—but it appears that such protections are not full proof."

"What do you mean?" I asked, my curiosity growing.

"When I had finished, I had placed my clothes in the laundry basket without thinking. When I went to wash them an hour later, I just picked them up, not realizing that the juice from the poison ivy plant would still be on them and could still get on your skin just from the briefest of contact. And so, here I am." She showed me her arm with the red, blistery rash.

"Well, I hope this stuff helps," I told her and started to leave.

"Funny thing, isn't it," she said, "how something invisible like that can stay on your clothes, waiting to strike the next time you put them on."

An idea formed in my mind as I started to remember something from a high school English class. Wasn't there a story about someone who was poisoned by putting on clothing that had been soaked in something lethal? I grinned at the woman and wished her a good day as my mind remained focused on this detail it refused to remember. Sneaking away and hiding behind some candlesticks, I pulled out my phone and launched its web browser, typing in "poisoned clothes" in the search bar. Over 600,000 results popped up and among them were:

The Arsenic Dress
Poisoned Clothing of the 19th Century
Medea's Revenge

That's it! That was the story I tried to remember. Medea, a woman from the ancient Greek mythology, who was married to Jason, but he left her for another woman, the King of Corinth's daughter. So, she sent a dress and coronet, covered in poison, to the woman, thus killing her when she put it on. In some versions two of Medea's sons died as well when they touched the poisoned garments.

I did not have time to do much research on my phone, and after a while the small screen made my eyes hurt from staring at for too long. I needed a better place to research my hunch. I glanced at the clock. Noontime. Perfect. My lunch hour had arrived. I found Jackie at the register, finishing up with a customer.

"Do you mind if I take my lunch now?" I asked her.

"Go ahead," she replied.

"You're in charge while I'm gone," I told her and she gave me a "duh" look. "And find a way to keep Tammy busy. I don't need any mishaps today."

"Oh, I got you covered on that one." The devilish grin on Jackie's face made me glad that I was not Tammy.

As I left the shop, I texted Greg, asking him if he could meet me at the library and he replied that he would take his break early and be right there. I loved him. I arrived at the library within minutes, glad that there wasn't a lot of traffic and that I had been able to get there quickly. He stood in front of the entrance as I pulled up.

"So, what do you need?" he asked me as I walked up to him and gave him a kiss.

"What makes you think I need something?" I teased.

"You always call when you need something."

Okay. Okay. He had me there. "I don't have a lot of time and I needed to look something up. Stuff about poisoning through contact with clothes."

"You still think she was murdered?" he asked me.

"It's starting to look like she could have been."

He opened the door for me and we went inside. I took a quick glance at the circulation desk, but did not see the old woman there. Maybe this was her day off. She did say that she volunteered, so perhaps she showed up when it was convenient for her.

"Let's each take a computer and search for anything about using clothes to spread a contact poison," I suggested.

"Good idea."

I sat at one of the card catalog computers and Greg took the one next to me. Rattling my brains for a search term, I typed in the first thing I thought of: Medea. A lot of books appeared, but I needed one that was a bit more narrowed down, so I typed Medea, poison. One book came up titled, *Jason, the Argonauts, and Medea's Revenge.* That could be useful. I looked up its location and wrote it down on a piece of paper that the library always kept near their catalog computers.

Next, I typed contact poisons in the search bar and waited. A few books showed up: *Thinking of Murder?*, *Contact Poisons and their Uses*, *Poisoning of the 19h Century*, and *The Poisoned Wedding Dress*. The last one was a fiction novel, so I disregarded it. The first one seemed intriguing. Thinking of murder... always, but not in the way you might think. I wrote down the locations for the other books and added them to my list.

I glanced at Greg and he showed me his small list of books to look at, so I pointed at a nearby table and mouthed the words "I'll meet you there."

He nodded.

I roamed through the shelves, heading to the second level for where the books I searched for were located. I found the one about Medea in the history section, buckling under the weight of the 11x15 book, making me rethink my decision to carry it all the way back to the floor level of the library. I had to head to the third level for the other two, where the crime, thriller, and real life cold case mystery books were kept, finding them and adding them to my pile, afraid that I might drop all the books as my arms strained to carry them all.

I hurried down the stairs and to the table where I asked Greg to meet me and plopped my books on its surface, creating a tremendous bang, and garnering a few glares and SHHH's in response. "Sorry," I mouthed to some unforgiving stares as I opened the book on Medea.

Greg appeared, carrying his own armful of hardbacks, but he placed them on the table with more care than I did, much to my relief. "Well, I found a few things."

I opened the book about Medea and her revenge, flipping to the pages that concentrated on how she got her revenge with Jason after he left her. Skimming the pages, and admiring the artful and vibrant illustrations that accompanied the text, I refreshed my memory about the entire myth. Medea had helped Jason steal the golden fleece and he married her in return, after which, she bore him children. After about ten years, in some versions of the myth it was longer or shorter, Jason left her for the daughter of the king of Corinth, and as a woman scorned, she vowed to get revenge. Here is where I give the woman props for being creative, even if it was vindictive and cold: Medea sent Jason's new bride a wedding gift of a dress and golden coronet, or crown, which had both been doused in poison. When the princess and her father touched the garments, they died. I just wish the book told me what poison Medea had used.

Flipping more pages, I realized there were more versions of the story. In another one, Medea murdered two of her children as a way of exacting her revenge against her husband. Now that is just cold. I skimmed through a few more passages, but concluded that the book on Medea's method of committing murder, though interesting, wouldn't give me what I needed: real life cases where people used a poisoned item to commit murder.

"Find anything?" I asked Greg.

"A few things," he replied. "Have you ever heard of the arsenic dress?"

"The what?"

"In the nineteenth century, arsenic was used to create the green color which many clothes were dyed in. And not just the clothes, but women's headdresses as well. The green dye was so toxic, that many wealthy women in Britain, France, and North America died from it. And the green coloring wasn't just used in clothing, but in wallpaper and textiles—almost anything."

"Good, grief," I said. "How did people survive?"

"Good question."

"But those deaths were all accidental," I said.

"Doesn't mean that someone couldn't have gotten the idea of dousing an article of clothing in arsenic in order to commit murder."

True. "Maybe we should look up contact poisons."

"Just about any poison can be administered by contact, but most of your poisons are most effective if consumed orally."

"But what about the missing scarf?" I asked.

Greg gave me a doubtful look, since I seemed to be the only one who remembered Melanie Sanders wearing a scarf that day, but in an effort to humor me, he brought out another book and opened it. "Cyanide can be administered through contact, but as an inhalant. You use its powder form, and put in on something that the intended victim would sniff. Arsenic can also work as a contact agent, but it is more deadly if ingested."

I frowned. If the woman had been poisoned, she would had to have consumed it, but none of that explained the missing scarf. Considering the way it was wrapped around her throat, the wind could not have just blown it away. Someone had to have taken it, but why? A sinking feeling that I focused in the wrong direction settled over me as I questioned my own conclusions.

"Look," said Greg, "the scarf may just be a scarf, and a red herring at that. Besides, we don't know for sure if she was poisoned."

Another problem. "What does Jack have to say about that?"

Greg smiled. "I thought you would never ask."

He pulled out his phone and a set of ear buds, handing me one of the buds while he stuck the other in his ear before plugging the buds into the audio jack of his phone and dialing Jack. The phone rang and went straight to voice mail. Greg called him again. For a second time, it went straight to voice-mail. By the third instance, I knew that the man avoided us.

"I have a feeling he doesn't want to talk to us," I said.

"You're getting that impression too, huh?"

"Text him and tell him that I'll send Tiny over if he continues to ignore us."

One Halloween, I had tried to call Jack about an unsolved murder I had gotten myself involved in, with Rachel's help, and he refused to talk to me. So, I had just called Tiny and asked him to persuade Jack to take my phone call. Jack still has not forgiven me for that.

Greg sent the text and within a minute his phone rang. "Jack, how nice of you to call," he said in a cheery voice, garnering a few hushes from some nearby patrons who were unhappy about their quiet time at the library being interrupted by someone's cell phone ringing.

"What do you want?" demanded Jack.

"Has the toxicology report for that woman who died on the fourth come back?" asked Greg.

"You mean the pageant girl?"

"Yes."

"Why?"

"I need to know how she died."

"Why?" Jack repeated.

"Because Mel thinks that something isn't right."

"Your girlfriend always thinks that something isn't right."

"My girlfriend," said Greg, his voice growing tight, "is listening in on this conversation with her hand ready to send Tiny a message."

"Jack please," I added, hoping that being a bit more friendly would get better results.

"Give me a minute," said Jack.

Silence ensued as we waited, and I listened to the clacking of the keys on the other end, growing impatient as I realized what time it was and how I needed to get back to work. "Jack?"

"Got it," he replied. "Her stomach contents consisted of water, orange juice and a few raisins. Geez, doesn't anybody eat anymore?"

A mental image of Jack munching on some fries and a burger as he talked to us floated through my mind.

"According to this," Jack continued, "she had something called ricin in her system. The coroner was unable to determine how she got such high levels in her system."

"Ingested?" asked Greg.

"It can be administered orally and more tests are being done on the small amounts of food that was still undigested in her stomach, but that wouldn't account for the amount found."

"How much was in her system?" asked Greg.

"About sixty milligrams," Jack replied.

"Thanks Jack. Keep us informed of any new developments."

Jack mumbled a few foul words before we were able to hit the hang up icon on the phone.

Greg pulled one of the books he had found about poison closer to him and flipped through the pages with such fervor, that I was afraid he might tear one. I watched him with confusion, wondering what had possessed him to act in such a manner. My question was soon answered as he shoved the book in front of me, pointing to a specific page that listed some of the more deadly poisons: VX nerve agent, discovered in the 1950s; batrachotoxin, a toxin that comes from the skins of tiny frogs in South America; arsenic, most commonly known and used in the 19th century; maitotoxin, which comes from marine life; and ricin, which comes from the castor oil plant.

Greg's finger rested on the passage about ricin and I read over it. Castor oil comes from the beans of the plant itself and is extracted, but what remains in the solid fibers is the compound known as ricin and it is very deadly. According to the book, only 20 milligrams are needed to cause death and Melanie Sanders had three times that amount. What did she do to force someone to go to such lengths to kill her?

"It says here," I repeated the line of text, "that it is most deadly when consumed orally or injected into the bloodstream."

"So much for your theory about contact poisons," said Greg.

"So how did she get it?"

"My guess is the raisins. Jack said that those were the only things found in her stomach, other than orange juice."

"So, it could have been in the juice too," I mused.

"Possible," Greg replied, "but that would be the more logical explanation for how she was poisoned. We'll know more, when Jack gets back to me on the results of the lab tests on her stomach contents."

"Are you sure he'll call you?"

"Oh, he will. He's not going to want our mother to know that he missed her birthday because he had decided to go windsurfing instead."

"You're such a blackmailer," I teased.

"The best."

I leaned in to kiss him, but stopped when the librarian hushed us. Her cross look could have petrified Medusa. I checked the time and jumped from my seat. "Hate to research and run, but..."

"I know. Have fun at work."

I chuckled, still wondering what plan Jackie had come up with to keep Tammy out of trouble when I remembered her little surprise. "I'm afraid you'll be on your own for supper tonight."

"Oh?"

"Jackie entered me into that beauty pageant that takes place this weekend."

"Really? So, you agreed to this?"

"No," I said. "She forged my signature, but it is the best way to poke around."

"Is there a swimsuit competition?" Greg joked.

"Probably," I replied, picking up the books I had gotten off the shelf, "and don't go getting any ideas."

I took my books to one of the reshelving carts near the table we had sat at and left the library, receiving an unfriendly glare from the librarian. Give it a rest, lady. We weren't any louder than the teenagers laughing over pictures that one of them had posted on their social media page. Once out of the building, I hurried to my car, knowing that I had just enough time to get back to work and learn what mischief Jackie and Tammy had been up to.

I slammed my car door shut as I jumped out and ran down the sidewalk to the Candle Shoppe, squeaking in with one minute to spare only to find Jackie standing there at the counter with her phone out and the stopwatch app ticking down the seconds. "You're timing me?" I asked her, incredulous.

"Cutting it close," she said. "Okay, okay, I'm just joking with you, but you were cutting it close and I'd like to eat too."

"Sorry," I apologized, "but Greg and I found some interesting stuff at the library."

Jackie leaned closer, but I realized that I didn't see Tammy anywhere.

"Where's Tammy?" I asked.

Jackie motioned for me to follow her and I did, allowing her to take me to the back office. I couldn't believe it. Tammy was on all fours, scrubbing the tile floor with a... toothbrush? I faced Jackie and she read my unspoken question. Instead of answering me right there, since Tammy hadn't noticed our presence, she pulled me out to the main room.

"I needed something that would keep her busy and these floors have been looking a little grungy, so I decided that this was how I could keep her occupied."

"A toothbrush?"

"It's what they do in the Marines," protested Jackie.

"Maybe, but where did you find a toothbrush?"

"Mr. Stilton's office. Hopefully he doesn't actually brush his teeth with it."

"And she willingly went along with this?"

"No, but I can be persuasive," answered Jackie. "She's a fast worker too, when she puts her mind to it. She already has about a quarter of the back room done and it looks a lot shinier back there."

I couldn't believe it. At least, we might get a few bonus points for getting the back storeroom cleaned out, something it has needed for the last few years.

"Spill," said Jackie. "I want to know what you found out."

Before answering, I glanced around to see if any customers were nearby to overhear us, but the store was almost empty with only two other people there shopping. It shaped up to be a quiet afternoon. "We called Jack and learned that Melanie had eaten some raisins and orange juice within hours before dying and her lab work comes back positive for poisoning."

"Poison?"

"Ricin," I said.

Jackie gave me a quizzical look and I explained that it came from the castor oil plant.

"So, the scarf, assuming she had been wearing one, had nothing to do with it," said Jackie.

"Seems so, and I was certain that—"

"She had been wearing one." Tammy stood in the doorway to the backroom, dangling the muck infested toothbrush by her side.

"How long have you been standing there?" I asked, wondering if this was what it felt like to have your private conversation with a friend listened in on by someone else.

"Only a minute," replied Tammy. "Can I stop now? My arm is getting really tired."

Jackie crossed her arms and I know she debated between telling Tammy to just use the other one or letting her rest. I gave her a pleading look and she relented. "Go ahead and take five."

Pleased, Tammy walked over to her bag, placing the toothbrush on the counter and grabbed her phone from her purse. "She had been wearing a scarf."

Tammy handed us her phone, showing us a picture of Melanie Sanders on the stage, wearing a matching scarf to her dress, complete with the two white daisies on it. She scrolled through more pictures (how many of the pageant did she take?) and I knew that I had been correct. Melanie had worn a scarf on stage when she died, but it was now missing. It may not be responsible for her death, but someone wanted to make certain that the police never found it.

"And," said Tammy with a proud grin, "I saw someone wearing an orange dress that day."

I frowned at her. She had never mentioned it before and a part of me wondered if this latest confession from her had more to do with what I had found in the culvert yesterday, and not what she had actually witnessed. "Does it match the cloth I found yesterday?"

"Yes!"

"Tammy, you're making it up."

"No, I'm not!" Her tone was too defensive and I wondered if perhaps she had made up her little story about the sewers and had just gotten lucky.

"Do you have any pictures of this woman?" Jackie asked.

Tammy pulled her phone closer to herself. "No," she mumbled.

"Perfect," quipped Jackie. "I'm going to lunch. Have fun with her."

Soon after Jackie grabbed her purse and left, my phone buzzed, informing me that I had just received an email. "Tammy, why don't you take care of the register."

She beamed and skipped across the room to the counter, her hair waving behind her. I opened my email app and learned that the man I had emailed last night had replied.

Miss Summers,

I received your message and am intrigued about your interest in local Vermont history, particularly the Beaumont heir. Yes, I would be delighted to meet with you. I have a local address: 6376 Fairmont Drive. Does 9am work?

William Nunche

www.williamnunche.com

He wanted to meet with me! Good. Perhaps I could get some answers about this old family of Vermont and who Melanie Sanders really was. I opened up my web calendar and added the appointment to meet with Mr. Nunche at nine in the morning after sending him a reply, telling him that the chosen time was fine. I just hoped that he would be able to give me more information than what was on his website.

"Look out!"

Startled, I turned just in time to watch as Tammy plowed into me, carrying an oversized box that her muscles strained to carry, knocking me over. We both sprawled on the floor while the box tumbled out of Tammy's arms, spilling its contents everywhere. I watched, helpless, as my phone flew from my hands, smashing into the side of a shelf and the back popped off while pieces of it scattered on the carpet. Really! My phone survived drowning in a sewer just to get busted open from someone knocking it out of my hands? AARRRGH!

I glared at Tammy and she must have seen murder in my eyes because she shrank away.

"Sorry!" she said.

"Weren't you supposed to stay by the register?" I asked her, my voice tight as I tried to control my anger.

"Yeah, but," began Tammy, "I noticed that some of these candle sticks had been sitting in the back and I thought that if I put them out there were could sell them."

"Tammy, those were the candle sticks that Mr. Stilton had wanted to send back because they were defective. See?"—I held three of them up—"they all aren't the same length."

"I'm sorry, Mel," wailed Tammy, feeling bad, "I just—"

"Just put them back," I said, trying not to yell at her as I picked up my phone and its back, hoping I could just pop it back on and unenthused about the prospect of having to purchase a new one if it didn't work.

Tammy cleaned up the candlesticks and ran to the backroom and I think I saw a few tears well up in her eyes. Good one, Mel, I scolded myself, you've hurt her feelings and she was just trying to help.

The bell on the door jingled and Jackie walked in, back from her lunch break. "What happened?" she asked, noticing me sitting on the floor.

"Tammy," I mouthed.

Jackie nodded and put her purse away before stepping behind the register to assist a few customers.

The rest of the afternoon passed without incident, but my conscience would not leave me alone as it badgered me for being so curt with Tammy. Once the last customer had left, I went to the backroom where Tammy had spent the rest of the day sulking and, as it turned out, organizing the boxes that were stored back there.

"Tammy," I said.

She refused to look at me.

"Tammy, I'm sorry I yelled at you. I realize that you were just trying to help."

"I'll replace your phone," she said, her voice low.

"I'm not worried about that. I… did you do all this?" I studied her handiwork a little closer, realizing that she had catalogued the inventory in the back, placing the candles together, according to their type, the warmers were in another section, organized by occasion and color, while our incense had been grouped together according to the scent they released and function. Impressed, I had the feeling that we might actually be able to find stuff back here. Mr. Stilton wasn't always good at organizing. He tended to just throw newly arrived orders back there with a "I'll get to it later" attitude.

"I just wanted to be alone, but I got bored so…"

"Tammy, this is good work. You might be better suited to help us keep track of our inventory."

"You think so?" Her eyes lit up.

"I'll mention it to Mr. Stilton."

Tammy's mood perked up.

"Anyway, it's closing time and Jackie and I need to get going. If you want, you can finish up here and…"

"Where are you going?"

"We were going to try out for that pageant thing," I replied.

"Oh!" Tammy jumped up and down with excitement. "Can I join? Oh, but I still have a few boxes to put away."

"I think they are accepting applications up until seven tonight, which is an hour from now. Here's the key. If you're quick, I'm sure you'll make it in time. Just remember to lock up and give me the key back." I gave Tammy the key to the front door, something I would not do under normal circumstances, but I wanted to give her the benefit of the doubt.

Tammy took the key, smiling to herself and hugged me, which I never expected. "I won't let you down. I'll finish up here and... and... I won't let you down!" She turned back to her task and I left, finding Jackie standing by the door, tapping her foot with impatience as she waited for me.

"Ready?" she asked.

"Yes," I replied, "though I'm still a little upset that you signed me up for this."

"Oh, it will be good for you. You need to learn to wear something other than jeans and a -t-shirt all the time."

"How did you learn to forge signatures in the first place?" I asked her as we walked out the door.

"I get bored sometimes."

Chapter 7

Jackie and I walked through the double doors to the convention center and I stopped, not believing the amount of people there, and feeling a little overwhelmed. Carts of fancy dresses rolled past us, pushed by someone wearing clothes similar to mine and each with a walkie talkie hanging from their belts and unhappy expressions on their faces. Ahead of me was a long table with people seated there, each looking a little haggard and annoyed as they took down names and passed out packets filled with important papers.

"There are a lot of people here," I said. "How many signed up for this thing?"

"There are only 55 contestants," replied Jackie, "but you also have makeup specialists, choreographers, the main spokesperson who will ask all the questions and make announcements, TV crews, costume designers… you know, all that stuff."

"Television crews?"

"Yeah, it's going to be aired live on channel five."

Jackie forgot to mention that part.

"I don't think I can do this," I said as I watched some of the women lining up to be a part of the show with their hair and makeup done to perfection with no flaw or hair out of place, much like Jackie's, while I stood there with my hair pulled back in a braid and only cover up on my face. I didn't even bother with mascara this morning.

"You'll do fine," Jackie said to me, pushing me towards the long table.

"Is it too late to back out?"

"Do you want to solve Melanie's murder or not?"

That did it. Jackie knew me too well. Of course, I wanted to solve Melanie Sanders' murder, but right now, I'd face a psychotic killer any day over these ladies. We strolled up to the table and signed in.

"Name?" asked the woman sitting there.

"Mellow Summers," I said.

The woman chuckled.

"You find my name funny or something?" I challenged her, not liking the way she laughed at it. Jackie, tapped my shoulder and shook her head, pleading with me to not let Tiny's influence get the better of me.

"Sign here," said the woman.

I signed the tablet she gave me and handed it back to her, receiving a packet in return.

"You agree and understand that the dresses are not owned by you, but by the city. You agree to replace any damaged property loaned to you. No pictures or video recordings are allowed in the changing area. Only authorized personnel are allowed back there which means no boyfriends, girlfriends, family members, or any other significant others. You are required to be here at least an hour before show time. Failure to comply will result in you being disqualified as a contestant. Do you understand and agree to these rules as I've presented them to you?"

I nodded, having missed most of what she said since she spoke fast and in a bored monotone, indicating that she had probably recited these rules too many times to count.

She pushed another tablet to me and I signed my name. "Next!" she called as I walked away and Jackie gave her name, received a packet, listened to the same set of rules, and signed the tablet when asked.

"Someone needs a new job," Jackie muttered to me, opening her packet and pulled out a few forms and instruction along with a badge, attached to a string, with the number 37 on it.

I opened mine as well and learned that I am number 38. "Now where to?"

Jackie read the schedule and pointed up the stairs. "The changing rooms are on the third level, but right now, we need to be in room two-twelve for lessons in poise."

"Poise lessons?" I checked the schedule and that was exactly what they were called. I guess it really is a thing.

We headed up the stairs and found room 212, where the other contestants were and I felt way out of place.

Most of the women glared at me and not Jackie. It was evident that she fit right in with her fashion forward clothes, her hair styled in such a way that it framed her face, and her makeup accentuated every aspect of her natural beauty, while I just stood there in my normal, everyday wear.

"The cleanup crew meet downstairs," said one woman with golden-blonde hair in a condescending tone.

"I'm a contestant," I told her.

The woman laughed. "Guess they'll allow just anyone in."

As though to add credence to her statement, guess who showed up?

"Mel! Jackie! I made it!" Tammy burst into the room, waving her packet, and wearing her usual homemade attire, along with a pair of shoes that had buttons of varying colors and shades, glued to the sides.

The woman laughed at Tammy's outfit. Tammy's fashion sense may have bordered on the absurd, but I never publicly laughed at it.

"Who are you laughing at?" Tammy charged the woman and both Jackie and I struggled to hold her back

"You two just don't belong here," the woman said to both Tammy and me, unafraid of Tammy's actions, before turning to Jackie, "and if you're with them, then you're just as trashy as they are."

"Let her go," said Jackie, releasing her grip on Tammy.

"What?" I said.

"Let Tammy beat that blonde bi—"

"Tammy!" I said, interrupting Jackie and getting Tammy to calm down. "If you hit her now, you'll be disqualified from the contest."

Tammy stopped struggling and did the "I'll be watching you" sign, which scared me a little as I have never seen her act like this before.

"Yeah, go back to your mommy," mocked the woman.

I faced her and closed the distance between us. "I never said anything about after the pageant, bi—"

Just then, a man walked into the room, wearing exercise pants and a tank top, exposing his toned muscles, speaking in an accent I hadn't heard before. "Ladies, ladies, please, no fighting." He faced everyone in the room and the woman shrank to the back of the crowd. "Now, I am here to teach you all how to properly walk, so that you do not embarrass yourself, or us, on television while on stage"

"Why do I feel like I have just stepped onto the set of *Miss Congeniality*?" I whispered to Jackie.

"Please, no talking," said the man and I focused on him again as he strutted from one end of the room to the other, straight and tall, demonstrating how to walk with the proper posture. He pointed at one girl and she strolled across the room, receiving an approving glance. The woman who had challenged us was asked to demonstrate her stride and she did so with flying colors. Even I had to hand it to her. She had great posture and possessed that elegance that one would expect to see in a place like this.

"You"—the man pointed at Jackie and she stepped across the room, receiving his approval—"Good! Good!"

"You!" He pointed at me and this was where things went downhill. I walked across the room in my usual manner and he held out his arm to stop me. "No! No! No! You're all wrong!"

I glared at him, frowning.

"You should stand up straight and tall with pride. This is not *Jurassic Park*."

"And you're not Michael Caine," I retorted.

Frustrated by my lack of respect, the man circled around me, assessing my stature. "Your buttocks should be in line with your lower back! Your stomach should be in! Your chin up and your head held high!" He slapped my bottom, my stomach, and placed his hand under my chin, lifting it, corresponding with each of his statements. "And a few less cheeseburgers wouldn't hurt you either, dear."

That's it! I'm okay with someone telling me my posture might be poor, but calling me fat when I only weighed 148 pounds is going too far, and I was not here to be ridiculed by a guy wearing leggings. I pulled back my fist, but before I could strike, the strong grip of Detective Shorts had stopped me.

"That's not recommended," he whispered to me.

"May I help you?" asked the posture instructor.

"I'm here to see a Candace Williams," replied the detective.

The woman who had insulted Tammy, Jackie, and me earlier squirmed in the background.

"This is a class, you can't..." began the instructor.

Detective Shorts showed his badge. "I'm still conducting an ongoing investigation and since many of the girls here were also present when Melanie Sanders died, I need to talk to them about what happened."

"I'm not going anywhere," snapped the woman, whom I learned was now named Candace.

"Miss Williams," replied Detective Shorts, sounding

as though he had encountered this sort of behavior too many times in the past, "you can either talk with me out in the hallway, or I can take you down to the station. And believe me, you won't be able to participate in this pageant if I do."

His threat had the desired effect and she huffed as she stepped out into the hallway. Before he followed her out, Detective Shorts leaned in and whispered, "I'll be speaking with you, too. Later."

Busted. I knew he would never believe that I was here for fun.

"Ladies, come on," said our instructor, clapping his hands. "Back to the lesson please!"

I turned away from the doorway and rejoined the group, following the instructor's directions on how to have perfect posture, wondering just what sort of questions the detective asked the woman, and what her responses were in return.

I didn't have to wait long to find out why Detective Shorts wanted to speak with me. The class finished within ten minutes and as I walked out the door with Jackie and Tammy, I found him waiting for me. He waved me over and I asked Jackie and Tammy to wait for me, hoping that this little chat wouldn't take too long.

"Miss Summers," he said, "what are you doing here?"

"Participating in the local pageant," I replied, trying to sound innocent. His scowl told me that he did not believe me. "It was Jackie's idea. She always wanted to be a part of one of these things and I said that I would join her."

"And it has nothing to do with the fact that the murder victim had participated in a similar event."

I kept my mouth shut. If I had tried to answer, my ruse would be known and he already didn't believe me anyway.

"I thought so," he said, as though my silence confirmed his suspicions. "I suggest you watch your back. The murderer is not the only one whom you have to worry about."

"It's just a pageant," I said.

"Not to them," he replied, pointing at some of the other girls watching us. "They take this sort of thing very seriously and detest people like you."

Something deep down in the pit of my stomach agreed with him and a part of me regretted allowing Jackie to talk me into this thing, but she was also correct: this was the only way to investigate the other contestants. "Is there anything else?" I asked.

Detective Shorts shook his head and waked away.

I know what he wanted to do, but legally he could not stop me or Jackie from participating in a pageant that was open to the public. I walked over to Jackie and Tammy.

"What now?" asked Jackie.

"Home," I said, feeling tired. Tammy frowned, but I just didn't have to energy to do anything else today. "Sorry, Tammy," I said to her, "but it has been a long day."

She released a huff of air and stalked off, while Jackie and I headed for the car and left. Our first pageant showing was tomorrow evening, but we would have to be there at least an hour before show time to get ready, but, for now, I intended to get some sleep.

Chapter 8

Around four in the morning, I woke up, unable to get back to sleep. My mind kept thinking about the tunnels that Tammy and I had explored. How could someone escape in there and make it out without being noticed, and wearing such nice clothing and heels? I pondered it, considering all options in my mind. Jackie wore heels sometimes and she is able to move at a fast pace in them, something I could never do without tripping, falling, or twisting an ankle. I just couldn't imagine someone wearing heels and a dressing gown crawling through the sewers without getting filthy.

There was only one way to know if such a thing was possible, but Jackie wouldn't like it. I got up and knocked on her bedroom door. "Jackie?"

"Go away!"

"It's about the case."

"It's four am!"

More like four-fifteen. I bit my lower lip for a second, debating whether I should continue to bother her and decided that I would just let her sleep and called Greg instead, knowing he would be up since he had an early shift today.

"Morning, sweetie," he greeted me when he answered. "It's a bit early for you to be up."

"Can't sleep," I replied.

"Oh?"

"I keep thinking about that tunnel. How does someone run through a sewer wearing a formal dress and heels and in just a few minutes?"

"Um… that's a good question."

"There's no way someone could do it wearing those three-inch heels that some of the contestants wore."

"Of course, you can," said Jackie, standing in the hallway, having gotten up without my notice.

"Greg, I'm going to put you on speaker." I hit the speaker icon on my phone.

"Look, it is possible to run wearing heels and a dress," said Jackie.

"But wouldn't you fall or get stuck? The sewer if full of…"

"I know what it's full of," Jackie interrupted me.

"Why don't you run an experiment?" Greg suggested. "Go to the sewer. Dress in some heels and see how long it takes run through it."

"I guess I could…"

"I'll wear the heels," Jackie said. "You trip when wearing sneakers."

I heard a snicker on the other end of the line. "What?"

"Nothing," said Greg, clearing his throat. "So, it's a plan then, but I won't be able to join you."

I frowned, remembering that he had to work most of the day.

"I'll call Tiny and have him meet you," said Greg.

"I'm sure Mel and I can handle it," Jackie murmured.

"We might need his help just to get the manhole cover off," I whispered to her. "We'll be there in half an hour," I told Greg.

"Tiny will be there." Greg hung up.

I ran to my room and slipped on some jeans, an old shirt, and some boots. When I had gone back out in to the living room, Jackie waited for me, dressed in similar attire and holding a pair three-inch heels. "Ready?" she asked.

I nodded,

We took her car and reached the park just as the sun came up over the trees, in about 20 minutes. Tiny and some of his gang waited for us, just as Greg had promised they would, though I knew he'd be there. If there was ever a chance to cause mischief or misbehave, Tiny was game for it. Jackie parked out of the way and I hoped that our presence did not attract any unwanted attention. The park did not open until eight, but one of Tiny's men had been stationed at the gate, opening it for Jackie and me and closing it after we pulled in. I wasn't going to ask how they managed to get the padlock off.

Jackie and I walked up to Tiny. Sombrero and Elise were there as well. "Hey," I said.

"Your boyfriend called," said Tiny, "saying that you needed some help getting into the sewer."

A strange request, I know, but not the first time I had made one. "Yes. I have a theory."

Tiny and the others moved closer to hear me better.

"I don't think the woman died by accident," I said. "I think she was murdered and that her murderer took the method used to commit the crime and used the tunnel under this park to escape, only I don't think she did."

"You know it's a woman?" asked Tiny,

"Not many men wear expensive gowns and heels and participate in a beauty pageant," I replied.

"She could have used the sewer to escape," said Elise. "There's another manhole in the street over there."

"I don't think she escaped," I said. "There is a manhole here, but there is another over there and a drain large enough for a person to slip through nearby."

I showed them where the other entrances to the sewer were, explaining to them my adventure with Tammy and how I thought that the killer probably used the drain to escape and the manhole cover to come back unnoticed, or vice versa. "What I need," I finished, "is to run an experiment, timing how long it takes to run the tunnel."

"And here is where I come in," said Jackie, putting on the heels she had been carrying.

Tiny lifted the manhole cover off where I had come out of the sewer two days before when I had been here with Tammy and Sombrero proceeded to help Jackie onto the ladder when she stopped him, reminding him that the killer would have had to do this on her own. A car drove past on the road and we all turned, hoping that it wasn't a police officer responding to a call about vandals in the park. I wasn't sure how I would explain that to Detective Shorts.

"Ready?" I asked Jackie when the car disappeared.

She nodded,

"Go."

I started the stopwatch on my phone and she lowered herself onto the ladder, moving the cover back in place with ease, having no difficulty lifting it, further proving that this manhole got used the most by the city maintenance crew. I hurried over to the grate with the others and waited. Seconds seemed to take minutes. Just when I thought that she might have run into trouble, Jackie's hand appeared on the grate and she pushed it off with ease, meaning that the missing bolts had not been replaced yet, and crawled out. I stopped the timer.

"How long?" she asked, breathing a little hard.

I looked at the time. "One minute, twenty seconds." Not bad, if you think about it.

"A little long, don't you think?" asked Tiny.

"Thanks," breathed Jackie.

"Maybe," I said," but with all the commotion, I don't think anyone would have noticed a person missing for a minute. Where was your attention focused that day?"

"The dead girl," said Elise and the others nodded.

There was just one thing that bothered me: the orange cloth. I had found it caught on a bramble that did not lie in the path Jackie just ran when in the sewer. How would that piece of material get there if the killer never went in that direction? Unless she did and ran into the same difficulty Tammy and I had in getting that manhole cover off.

"What's wrong?" asked Jackie, noticing my frown.

"Remember that piece of cloth I found?" I asked her

and she nodded that she did. "Well, I found it tangled up in some brush that has blocked a portion of the sewer, but it's over in this direction. The only way it could have gotten there is if the killer had tried to flee to that manhole over there, but it took both Tammy and me to lift that one because it was stuck on there pretty tight."

"Probably never used," muttered Tiny.

He marched over to his bike, grabbed a crowbar, and went to the cover I pointed out to him. His muscles strained as he tried to lift it, but it refused to budge, even though Tammy and I had managed to move it two days ago. Tiny waved Sombrero over and together they pulled on it until it popped off.

"That was stuck on tight," said Tiny. "It seems to form a suction when its put in place and look at all this rust. This thing is never used. There is no way a woman moved this on her own."

"But how was it possible for her to move that one?" asked Elise.

Another good question. Even I didn't have much trouble with it. We all stared at each other with no answer to the puzzle, except for Jackie.

"Because they are redoing them."

"What?" I said.

"If you would read the local paper once in a while, you would know. There was an article a few months ago about how the city was redoing the manhole covers around town, making them from stronger, but lighter metals. It will probably take them two years to complete the project."

"Smarty pants," mumbled Tiny to himself.

"Jackie," I asked," would you be willing to run from this manhole cover to that one, wearing your heels?"

"I guess so," she replied.

Once again, she lowered herself into the sewer and I started the timer, hurrying over to the other cover where I waited for her. If I thought the time had dragged while awaiting her first run in the sewer to finish, then this one tested my patience to its breaking limit. Again, the seconds seemed like minutes while the minute seemed like hours. I tapped my foot as I waited, checking my phone's stopwatch every two seconds, growing worried the more it dragged. Unable to bear it any longer as the sun grew brighter and brighter the higher it rose into the sky, I leaned over the opening.

"Jackie?" I called.

No response.

Had something happened? Do I need to go down in there to get her? "Jackie?" I called again, louder.

"I'm here!" came her response from the bottom of the ladder.

Relief flooded over me and I rubbed my clammy palms on my pants leg. "I thought you got stuck or something," I said.

"A little, but nothing I couldn't handle."

Sombrero reached down and helped her out of the manhole.

"How long?" she asked.

"Four minutes," I said.

"Really?"

"Well, it was really three minutes forty-eight seconds. I rounded up."

"So, four minutes here and a minute and a half over

there," said Elise. "That's just over five minutes that someone would have been missing. Someone would have noticed."

"Again, where was all our attention focused?" I said. I know mine had been on the dead woman the entire time. I never thought to look around.

"Well, these shoes are ruined," said Jackie, taking off her heels and putting her flats back on. Though her shoes had gotten muddy, the rest of her remained free of it, unlike me when I had been down there and ended up getting coated in filth.

I wandered back over to the first manhole we had uncovered while Tiny and Sombrero recovered the one Jackie had just come out of. The stage had been near the manhole that had the easiest cover to lift. As I explored that section, I saw the unmistakable signs that a stage had been there and the impression from the supports had not worn away yet. I moved over to the grate. When I had come out of it two days ago, there were tents there that had not been taken down. Though gone now, the holes in the grass from the stakes still remained. If I were the killer, I would have used the manhole near the stage, the trees there would have helped provide some cover, and come out of the grate where I could easily slip into one of the changing tents.

"Didn't you say that the contestants would have two of everything. Like, two of the same dress and two of the same style of shoes?" I asked Jackie.

"Some would, yes," she replied, "but not all."

"But the city provides them," I said.

"The city provides the clothes for the pageant we are

signed up for, but some contestants will still bring their own custom-made stuff."

"Whoa!" said Tiny. "You're in a beauty pageant?"

My face turned red from embarrassment. So far, only Jackie and Greg knew, but now the cat was out of the bag. "Yeah," I said. "It was Jackie's idea. The first show is tonight."

"All right," Tiny said, clapping me on the back. "We're going." He pointed at Elise and Sombrero and I'm sure he intended to bring most of his crew, meaning I was in for an interesting night.

I looked at the time. "Jackie, we need to get going if we're going to get to work on time."

She checked her phone too and jumped.

"Thanks, again, guys," I said to Tiny and the others. "See you tonight."

"Oh, we'll be there," Tiny called after me as I followed Jackie back to her car. "In the front row!"

We had just enough time to stop by the apartment for quick showers—Jackie being the one who needed it most this time—change and run off to the Candle Shoppe for our shift. When we had arrived, the door was unlocked and Mr. Stilton sat in his office. I guess he decided to not take the day off. I went to the backroom and put my belongings in my assigned locker, finding Tammy back there polishing the floor.

"What are you doing?" I asked, curious.

"After cleaning up this room, I thought the floors in the main store could use a cleaning, but I wanted to make sure that this homemade cleaning solution would work first, so I'm testing it in here."

Wow. Another good idea from Tammy. Did she do a brain swap with someone? I had never seen her so diligent before or willing to do something, much less witness any of her ideas actually working. Remember the indoor fireworks fiasco? There are still a few scorch marks on the ceiling.

"Good idea," I said to her when my phone buzzed. I answered it.

"Mel, it's Jack."

Jack? I thought he would call Greg. "Yes?"

"Look, I got the info you wanted. I did a little digging and it turns out that Melanie Sanders had been blackmailing the judges."

"What?"

"It seems she was having difficulty winning any contests for the past two years. Then, her scores suddenly go up without any logical reason. Six months ago, one of the judges, a Michael Carson, had accused her of blackmail and went to the police, but the charges were later dropped. Now, if you don't mind, I have more important things to do."

He hung up and I ended up saying thank you to static. Blackmail? That is interesting and would be a motive for murder, but was it a judge who killed her, or an angry contestant? I received an alert on my phone reminding me of an appointment I had scheduled today. Oh, my goodness! I had forgotten about my meeting with Mr. Nunche! I ran out into the main store front and found Jackie by the register, glancing at a magazine while she waited for the two customers browsing the shelves to decide if they were going to purchase something or not.

"Jackie," I whispered to her, "can you cover for me? I forgot about that meeting with the guy who writes about local history."

Jackie glanced into the backroom, no doubt gauging whether Mr. Stilton would leave his office or not, before replying and handing me her car keys. "Go ahead and go. I don't think he's going anywhere today. I'll cover you either way."

I mouthed the words "thank you" to her while I looked up Mr. Nunche's address on my phone's GPS and ran out to her car. His house was on the other side of town, but the interstate turned out to be faster than expected since there wasn't much traffic to deal with. I pulled into his driveway with two minutes to spare and hoped he would not think that I had forgotten about our meeting as I squeezed in at the last second. Hurrying out of my seatbelt, I got out of the car, locked it, and ran to the door, doing my best to control my breathing so it wouldn't appear that I had been in a rush and knocked on the solid wood door that had a tiny glass square in the top center which allowed light through. It opened within seconds.

"Good morning," Mr. Nunche greeted me. "For a moment, I thought you might have forgotten about our little meeting."

I smiled, hoping that my embarrassment did not show through.

"Would you like to come in?"

"Thank you," I said, shaking his hand. "I'm Mellow Summers, but you can call me Mel."

"Yes, that is what your email said. You look familiar."

He shut the door and studied me for a moment. "We met at the…"

"Park? Yes."

"And now you are suddenly interested in local history."

I followed him through a narrow hallway to a sitting room filled with big, plush, black leather chairs on opposite sides of a red rug. Bookcases made up the walls and each shelf sagged under the weight of various books.

"Have a seat," he said, pointing at a chair and I sat down.

"I'm sorry if I seemed rude to you at the park. I was there to mostly eat and wander around."

"And now that a local heiress has died you are suddenly interested in local history," said Mr. Nunche, getting right to the heart of the matter and nixing the chit chat.

"Well, yes. I found your blog article on Melanie Sanders interesting. I never knew that she had been telling people that she was a member of the Beaumont family."

"Nothing new, really. People always pretend to be part of some 'old family' just to gain notoriety."

"Shame."

"Yes, well, not everyone can get it the way you do." Mr. Nunche placed an old newspaper in front of me. I looked down at it to find one of Jillian Modsen's articles glaring back at me. Will I ever escape her hatred for me?

"I guess it's time for me to go."

"Oh, don't bother. I looked you up the moment I received your email and guessed the reason for your visit."

"You don't mind?" I asked.

"I can't fault someone for wanting to know more about the history of the town or state that they live in.

Unfortunately, as you know from reading my article, Miss Sanders lied about being a Beaumont."

Mr. Nunche stood up and walked over to a cabinet, tucked away among the shelves of books, and unlocked it, pulling out a rolled piece of what looked like parchment, but was definitely thicker than your average piece of paper. He brought it over to a table and motioned for me to come closer as he unrolled it, revealing a family tree. "This took me years to make as I had to track down the information. Much of our history becomes lost from war, rivalries, apathy, and records being damaged from fire or just time. I researched each member of the Beaumont family starting with Louvel."

I studied the elaborate genealogy chart that he had made, running my finger down the lines of succession, marveling at the amount of time that had gone into creating this.

"As you can see, Louvel had children and those children had children, and so the line goes until you get here." He tapped his finger on Ramond Beaumont's name. "There is no evidence that there are any other Beaumonts related to this line. Ramond himself had no children. But I did research Melanie Sanders' genealogy."

"You did all this in just a couple of days?" I asked, looking at another chart he brought out, with Melanie's family tree.

"It wasn't difficult and I learned what I needed to know. Melanie Sanders was born in the next town over, it's about thirty miles from here. Her mother's name is Patricia Sanders. Never married. But if you follow the lines here, you'll notice that there is no Beaumont among them."

"So, Melanie did lie," I said.

"It would appear so."

"Why?"

"A variety of reasons," replied Mr. Nunche. "Many people think that if they pretend to belong to some sort of aristocracy, or that they can trace back their family lineage several generations to a particular individual, that they will receive some sort of prestige. It buys their way into the elite and privileged crowd. People in Europe have been doing this for centuries."

He walked over to a desk that I had not noticed before as it had been tucked under a window and blended in with the rest of the room. He snatched a piece of paper from it, bringing it to me and handing it to me. "Here is her mother's address."

"You're giving it to me?" I asked, surprised.

"Judging by your past history—that is not the only article about you in the paper—you will probably need it."

"Why would you do this?"

"That poor girl may have lied about her lineage, but she is dead now. She deserves to have the mystery of her death solved."

"Thank you," I said and started to make my way to the door.

"One other thing," Mr. Nunche said, stopping me. He grabbed a book off a shelf that seemed to hold multiple copies of the same book and handed it to me. "That will be twenty-six, ninety-nine."

I gaped at him. He was forcing me to buy his book as payment for speaking with me. Clutching the piece of paper in my hand that had the address of Melanie's mother, I decided that it was a fair trade and dug through my purse for 26 dollars and 99 cents. I ended up handing him 27 dollars instead. "Keep the change," I told him.

"Nice doing business with you," he said.

Sure was, you sly swindler. I get information. He gets a book sold.

I left through the front door, telling him good-bye as I made my way back to Jackie's car, tucking the book into my purse, thankful that I had purchased a big one for a change. Mr. Nunche watched from a window as I left and, out of politeness, I waved at him as I pulled out of his driveway. At least I had another lead to go on.

I glanced at the address that Mr. Nunche had given me. It wasn't far and I could be there in 30 or 40 minutes, but I did not want to just show up. I parked the car on the side of the road and pulled out my phone, looking up the address, hoping that a phone number would be attached to it. There was one. Good. Now I just needed to have a reason to see her, suspecting that she would not want to talk with some snoopy local girl who solves mysteries as a hobby. Though, it seemed to be more of a lifetime commitment.

Before I dialed Melanie's mother, I texted Jackie, asking her if there was any way she could cover for me today.

Why, she texted back.

Because I have the address for Melanie's mom and am trying to get her to meet with me.

Covered, she replied.

Thanks. I texted her.

Sucking in a huge lungful of air, I let it out as I tried to come up with a plausible reason for speaking with her. Just as I was about to dial her number, my phone buzzed, telling me that I had just received an email. Thinking it might be important, I opened the message to be greeted with a friendly reminder that there was a pageant show tonight and I needed to be there a minimum of an hour early, preferably three, signed by the showrunner herself: Miss Danvers.

An idea hit me.

I brought up the dial pad and called Melanie's mother, hoping that she would answer, hoping that I had the correct number, and hoping that she would speak with me. The phone rang on the other end and I tapped my foot against the floor of the car as I waited.

"Hello," said a somber voice.

"Patricia Sanders?" I asked.

"Yes. Who's calling?"

I took a breath. Here I go, fibbing 101. "Mrs. Sanders, this is Ms. Danvers from the Miss Belle pageant and I was wondering if I could speak with you about your daughter Melanie. It appears that she…"

"Oh, I knew this would bite her in the behind one day," moaned Mrs. Sanders, cutting me off.

"Excuse me?"

"Can't you people leave me alone? I lost my daughter and…"

"I'm terribly sorry, Mrs. Sanders, but it is important. I guess I can wait until it will be more convenient for you."

"It will never be convenient!"

Shoot! I just struck a nerve. This wasn't going to go

anywhere and guilt at pretending to be someone else just to get some information from her gnawed at me. "I will call back some other time."

"No!" Mrs. Sanders said into the phone, stopping me as I was about to hit the end call button. "I'm sorry. It's not your fault that this happened and I'm sure you just have a job to do. This is best done in person. Meet me at the Five Star Café."

"I can be there in forty minutes," I said.

"I'll get a table near the front." She hung up.

That could have gone better, but at least she agreed to meet with me. I looked up the café and realized that I could take the highway east out of town and just stay on it, since it turned into main street, which also happened to be the same road the café itself was on. Good. I did not want to get lost.

I drove into the café's parking lot 35 minutes later and groaned when I noticed that there were no spaces for me to park. Cruising the aisles, I spotted one that had just been vacated and just as I was about to pull in, someone on a motorcycle charged past, squeezing between me and the two other cars beside me, stealing the last available space. I slammed the brakes to avoid hitting him and rolled down the window.

"Excuse me!" I called to him. "Are you insane?"

He just stared at me, wondering why I was upset.

"You almost caused an accident, you idiot, as I was pulling into that space."

"Mine now, bitch." He stalked away, proud of himself, and went inside.

Gritting my teeth, I debated rear ending his bike, but my meeting with Patricia Sanders was more important, so I moved on, spotting a recently vacated space in the next row. Before another parking space thief could take it, I seized the slot and got out of my car, locking it as I hurried to the café.

The small building bustled with activity, filled with the sound of clinking silverware, food sizzling on the grill, and coffee makers brewing fresh pots of their coveted morning beverage. I spotted the motorcyclist. The temptation to walk over and punch him in the face hovered in front of me, beckoning me to give in to its summons. I started to, but stopped when I remembered my real reason for being here. Glancing around, I searched for a table near the front with an elderly woman sitting alone. I noticed two. Time to pick one and hope I'm right.

I headed for the one closest to me, but stopped when an older gentleman walked up and sat down, having just gotten back from the bathroom. By the way they interacted, I could tell that they were husband and wife and that I had almost made an embarrassing mistake. I spun on my heels and headed for the remaining table with a woman sitting alone.

"Mrs. Sanders?" I asked the woman.

"Ms. Danvers, I presume," the woman replied, her voice flat.

A pang of guilt at having to dredge up painful memories struck me, but I pushed it aside. I needed to know if anyone other than the judges she might have been blackmailing, would have a motive to kill Melanie. "I am sorry about your loss," I said, hoping my sincerity came through.

"I ordered coffee for you. Hope you don't mind."

"Coffee's fine," I said.

"So, what is this all about?" demanded Mrs. Sanders, getting to the point and not beating around the bush.

My tongue dried up as my mouth turned into its own version of the Sahara Desert. I'm afraid I hadn't thought about that part, nor had I spent time rehearsing my story once I got here. Okay, Mel, time to think of something and think of it fast. "Mrs. Sanders, I am here because it appears that Melanie had told the press some rumors about her being the last descendant and, or heir to the Beaumont family. Now, you can understand, with all this publicity, how this looks. We don't need the sensationalization of—"

"Are you kidding me?" Mrs. Sanders' voice carried across the café, attracting some unwanted attention and I sunk into my chair a little as prying eyes turned our way. She seemed a little embarrassed as well and glared at the woman in the booth next to us, forcing her to avert her eyes.

"Look, I know how this sounds," I said.

"Do you?"

I chewed my tongue as I changed tactics. "Mrs. Sanders, I am not trying to be insensitive, but we have other participants in the pageant—other girls who have mothers and whose futures hang in the balance if this isn't contained."

That seemed to have calmed her a bit as she settled down and her face changed from outright anger to understanding. "Well, I don't want to upset the other girls or be responsible for their future careers and reputations being tarnished because of this. I told Melanie to quit spreading lies."

"So, her stories were not true?"

"Of course not!" Mrs. Sanders reached for her coffee, but tipped her purse over in the process, allowing a tarnish and torn photograph to spill out of it. Before I had a chance to get a good look at the single girl in the picture, she scooped it up and shoved it back in her bag. "I told her to stop making stuff up. This all started when her father left. She wasn't known for making friends. I don't know where she heard about the Beaumonts, but, one day, she started telling everyone in school that she was descended from them. I guess it was a way to make herself feel important. I told her this would all come back to haunt her. We had a huge argument over it one day when she was seventeen and she left home then."

"And the pageants?"

"Melanie always loved fashion and dressing up. She watched the various Miss America pageants with such admiration that I knew she would try to be in one someday. I refused to let her participate in the various beauty contests that children are allowed to be a part of. Soon after she left home, she met her handler Ruth."

"Ruth?"

"You know her. Ruth Jeager."

"Oh, yes, of course," I said, filing the name away for later.

"She put a lot of ideas in Melanie's head and even encouraged her to keep promoting that lie about being part of the Beaumonts. It reached the point where Melanie believed her own lie."

"When was the last time you had talked to your daughter?"

"When she left home. I only knew what she was up to because sometimes she made the local paper or one of former friends would tell me, except Wendy."

"Wendy?"

"A former friend of Melanie's. A few weeks after she had left home, I heard the tragic news that Wendy had died in a car accident. Sometime after that, I received a torn photo of Melanie in the mail, with a note saying that I should have this, but I never heard from her personally."

I just sat there, listening to the woman talk.

"I don't know where I went wrong," lamented Mrs. Sanders.

"What do you mean?"

"I raised Melanie to be kind, but all she cared about was making it in the pageant world and winning those scholarships no matter what the cost. Maybe that's why they thought it was her."

"Who thought what?" I asked, intrigued.

"Two girls involved in a drunk driving incident, and Melanie gets…" her voice trailed off.

"What happened that night?" I asked.

Mrs. Sanders must have realized that she had almost spoken about something she had wanted to forget about and clamped her mouth shut.

"Wendy wasn't alone in the car that night, was she?" I asked.

"Is there anything else?" Mrs. Sanders snapped.

I let the matter drop and tried a different tactic. "Mrs. Sanders, do you know if Melanie was blackmailing any of the judges?"

"What?"

"There are rumors that she was and that this was how she kept winning. I know they are just rumors right now, but enough of the other contestants believe it and if they learn the truth, then that means…"

"That the media will as well."

"I'm really sorry. I shouldn't have brought it up."

Mrs. Sanders took another sip of her coffee. "I wouldn't be surprised if she had. Truth is, I did not know my own daughter in the end."

I glanced at my watch and realized that it had gotten late and that I needed to get back if I was going to make it to my first pageant show on time. "You have my sympathies, Mrs. Sanders, though I know that isn't much. I thank you for your time."

I rose from my chair, taking the check that the waitress had dropped off at the table and paid it, leaving a tip for her. As I walked outside and headed for my car, I noticed that the motorcycle was still parked in the space I had first tried to pull in when I entered the parking lot. Still incensed over his reckless actions, I marched over to it. Harley-Davidson. Of course, it was. Those are some of the best motorcycles you'll find in this country.

I glanced around to see if anyone watched me, but didn't notice anyone. Allowing my desire for revenge, and a little bit of Tiny's influence, to come out, I raised my left leg and kicked the bike, knocking it over. The sound of it landing on its side as it crashed in the parking lot made me cringe as it sounded louder than it probably was. I hurried to Jackie's car and drove away, taking the highway back to town and grinning to myself when I saw the man run out to his precious bike, cussing and stomping the ground as he inspected the damage. Maybe next time, he won't steal a parking space as someone is pulling in.

Chapter 9

I made it to the civic center just in time to rush through the front doors and up the stairs to the designated changing area where Jackie paced back and forth with her arms crossed, checking her phone every few seconds and sighing when I continued to not show. "There you are!" she said as I reached the top step, the belt of her bathrobe flinging from side to side as she turned. "Come on! We've got to get you dressed!"

I gaped at her, wondering why she wore a bathrobe.

"Come on!" Jackie shoved me into the chaotic room where other girls bustled about, combing their fingers through their hair, putting on their earrings, adjusting their... bikini tops? BIKINI TOPS? No one said anything about a swimsuit competition!

I turned and tried to run out of the room, but Jackie

seized my arms, flung me back around, and pushed me further into the maze of women with too much makeup on and all prancing around in heels and swimsuits. Before I had a chance to take everything in, I found myself shoved into a chair in front of a vanity mirror where I cringed as it showed every dimple and blemish on my face and alerted me to how tangled my hair had gotten. Jackie pulled the ponytail band out of my hair, allowing the strands to fall around my face. She snatched a brush and pulled at my tangles.

"Ow!" I screamed.

"Well, maybe if you had gotten here sooner, I'd have more time to be gentle," chastised Jackie.

"I'm sorry," I apologized, "but the chat with Melanie's mother took longer than expected."

Jackie stopped brushing my hair. "And what about that author guy? Did you meet with him?"

"I did," I replied. "He showed me the actual family tree for the Beaumont family that Melanie claimed to be descended from and she was nowhere on there. Then, he told me about her family lineage and the digging he had done into it, after looking through public records, he had located her mother, including her phone number, which he gave to me after he forced me to buy his book."

Jackie chortled at that one. "Forced you?"

"He basically shoved his book into my hands and wouldn't let me leave until I gave him money for it."

Jackie laughed again. "So, you called the mother?"

"Yes, and she agreed to meet with me in the next town over. She doesn't live very far."

"What did she say?" Jackie asked as she styled my hair for me.

"Pretty much what we suspected. Melanie had made the whole thing up while still in school. Her father had left, I'm assuming when she was young, and I guess she wanted to feel important. After a while, she seemed to believe her own lie. Either way, she stuck with her story and used it as a way to get in with this crowd."

"I don't know how that would work," said Jackie. "Some of these people are real…"

"Oh my gosh!" Candace Williams stalked up to us and laughed at my hair. "You aren't even dressed yet? And look at your hair! It's a mess!"

Jackie's face contorted as she curled the ends of my hair.

"You shouldn't waste your time with her," Candace said to Jackie. "She obviously won't win anything. Will probably get kicked out after this first round."

I noticed Jackie's expression change. It transformed into the same one she always got when she planned to do something devious, something that wasn't like her, except when someone angered her enough.

"Those cheekbones are too high and your clothes"— Candace picked at my shirt—"are too manly."

In a split-second, Jackie turned and held the curling iron against the woman's swimsuit until smoke formed.

"What the"—Candace jumped back with a shocked and furious look on her face. On her bikini top was a black mark where the curling iron had touched it and melted the fabric. "Look at what you've done!"

"If you can't take the heat, then maybe you shouldn't stand too close," Jackie retorted as she continued to curl the last bits of my hair, giving it some soft waves.

Candace fumed and stormed away, tugging at her bikini top in a vain attempt to get the burn mark out of the fabric.

"Good luck finding a new one," Jackie muttered to herself before turning back to me. "Okay, Mel"—she dumped a bunch of makeup in front of me—"it's time to get you all beatified."

"Where did you get all this?" I asked, recognizing the powder I usually wore and the mascara—the extent of my makeup routine in the morning.

"I had Greg bring it with him, and I picked up a few extras, when he gave me a ride here."

I had forgotten that I had been using her car. "I'm so sorry!"

"Don't worry about it," said Jackie as she touched up my concealer and applied eyeshadow and eyeliner to my eyes, making them pop. "At least you learned something."

"Mrs. Sanders wasn't too happy about her daughter making up stories and she implied that she wouldn't be surprised if Melanie had been blackmailing the judges. She said her daughter had huge ambitions and she didn't agree with her methods. So, they stopped talking to one another."

"Harsh."

"Come on, girls! Last call!" The stage manager shouted in an effort to round us all up. "Number thirty-seven you're up in five!" she yelled at Jackie.

Jackie whipped around and nodded at the stage manager, before turning back to me. "Okay, here is your lip gloss. I trust you know how to put it on. And here is your swimsuit." She handed me a garment bag. "Just remember to put these on first. They're sanitary liners."

I held up one of the see-through panties—at least,

I think they were panties, but smaller and tighter—and gave Jackie a questioning look.

"You can't wear your normal underwear with the swimsuit. So, put these on first, then the swimsuit, and, if you need them, there are tampons in my bag. And don't forget the shoes!"

That part of my life ended last week, so I was good to go for another four and didn't need to search through her bag for the feminine items—thank goodness.

"Thirty-seven!" yelled the stage manager.

"See you in a bit." Jackie ran off to take her place on stage.

Sighing, I applied the lip gloss, being careful not to spread it beyond the edges of my lips and unzipped the garment bag to reveal the swimsuit that had been loaned to me for this competition: a bikini. Of course, it was. At least they gave me a nice coral color which brought out the highlights of my hair. I found a privacy screen to change behind and ran to it, knowing that soon I would be called to the stage, and took my clothes off, until I was naked. Grabbing the sanitary liner, as Jackie had called it—I gave it another pessimistic look before pulling it on—not liking how it fit way too snug against my bottom, but guessed that it was supposed to. At least its see-through nude color made it practically invisible, which must have been the point. I put on the swimsuit, amazed that it fit so well before snatching the tag with my number on it and pinning it to the front of my top.

A bit of glitter caught my attention and I turned towards it. Heels. My old nemesis. I detested wearing them, always preferring shoes that were flat and laced up because those stayed on your feet and you didn't trip over them. But there was no escaping the heels this time. I grabbed the sparkling, silver shoes and put them on, using a nearby table to help steady me as I stood up. Did they have to be so high? What are these? Four inches?

As I made my way back to the table Jackie had parked me in front of, I spotted a trophy with Melanie's name on it shaped like a crown. I picked it up and studied it, wondering why it was here until I noticed a piece of paper, it's bottom corners covered with tubes of lipstick and eyeliner. Since no one was around, I picked it up and read what had been written on it. It was an application to the Vermont State Beauty Pageant, except Melanie's name was not on there and the participant and the application was dated a week before her death.

"What are you doing?" demanded an irate woman and I jumped a little, having not heard her come in.

"What is this?" I asked, holding up the application.

"None of your business!" snapped the woman.

I studied her face, knowing I had seen her somewhere before and it clicked. She had been the one who had helped Melanie adjust her scarf before she took the stage that day in the park. "You were with that murdered girl."

The woman's face reddened even more. "I was her manager, not that it's any of your business."

I glanced at the other name on the application where it asked for the contestant's manager's signature. "So, you're Ruth Jeager? But Melanie's name is not the one on this application for the Vermont State Beauty Pageant."

She reached for the application, but I held it just out of reach.

"It's a bit odd," I said.

"Not at all. Managers change contestants all the time."

"Except this is dated last week and usually the former contestant doesn't die."

"What are you implying? Give me that!"

Ruth reached for the paper, but before I could do anything, Tammy appeared out of nowhere and tackled the woman, forcing her into the vanity and creating a tremendous crash.

"I've got your back, Mel!" shouted Tammy as she wrestled with Melanie's former manager.

"Tammy, stop!" I yelled at her.

Tammy let go of the woman and allowed her to stand up.

"Are you insane!" screamed Ruth.

Ignoring her question, I asked her one of my own. "Your former contestant is now dead and here is an application with another's name on it with last week's date on it. It looks a bit suspicious and if it were to fall into the hands of the police, I'm sure—"

"All right! Melanie had become too much of a handful. She had been ill off and on and chewed me out when I had asked her if she was pregnant."

"Ill?"

"Nauseous and vomiting some. The typical symptoms of morning sickness. Of course, she insisted she wasn't, but her illness had definitely made her more moody than usual. And God forbid anyone saw that scar of hers."

"Scar?" I asked.

"She had a scar on her neck which was why she always wore a scarf. I was always readjusting her scarves for her to hide that scar. Got it in some accident, but she never talked about it. And then, she wouldn't stop going on about how she was descended from some famous family. I know there is a lot of backbiting in these sorts of competitions, but her insistence at belonging to some important family wore on me and the other contestants. Besides that, her scores had been low for the last two competitions she had been in. Then, out of nowhere her scores improve and are better than the other girls'. I know cheating when I see it and I confronted her. She didn't have to say it outright, but her actions told me that she was blackmailing one of the judges and I wanted nothing to do with it. We both agreed to part ways."

"And your new contestant?" I asked.

"Is no longer mine," replied Ruth. "Ever since Melanie died, I have become persona non-grata and my new protégé has found someone else to manage her. I just found out tonight and was coming back here to pack up some of my stuff."

"Thirty-eight," the stage manager walked into the room, "you're up."

I gave the application back to Melanie's former handler and apologized, not that it mattered at this point, before turning to Tammy. "What are you doing back here? I thought you were supposed to be on stage."

"I was disqualified from this round because no one liked the modifications I made to my outfit."

For the first time, I noticed Tammy's swimsuit. She had added tassels with fish fins hanging from them that swayed with the slightest movement. "It's against the rules, you know."

"Their outfits are so plain," whined Tammy.

"Thirty-eight!"

I ran out of the room, knowing that the stage manager was probably ready to murder someone after having to nag the contestants over and over to get out on the stage. I hurried to the auditorium as best I could, but the heels I wore threatened to get caught in the carpet and force me to trip, not that it would have been difficult.

"This way!" The stage manager grabbed my shoulder and forced me to go through a side door to the auditorium that led to the stage, instead of the main room, which was where I had been headed. I entered backstage, walking past the other contestants who waited to be called out, noting that Candace had managed to find a new swimsuit. She glared at me, but I ignored her.

"And introducing contestant number thirty-eight," announced the announcer. "Mellow Summers!"

I took a deep breath and stepped onto the stage into the stream of light, still holding the air in my lungs. As I started to get a little fuzzy, I realized that I had never exhaled, so I released my breath, sucking in another one soon after. The roar of the crowd and applause thundered in my ears, but seemed to be drowned by my own heartbeat. I headed for the center of the stage where the announcer waved me over, probably wondering why I took so long to walk out there.

Out of nowhere, a huge ruckus of cheers and applause filled the auditorium, followed by a series of whistles. I glanced in the direction of the noise and spotted Elise sitting next to Tiny and Greg with the rest of his men taking up the entire row.

"Tell us your name," said the announcer, which seemed redundant since he had already broadcasted it to the audience.

"Mellow Summers," I said, "but everyone calls me Mel."

"Well, Mel" he chuckled at that bit, thinking he had been clever in making up that little rhyme, "let's see those scores for this first round."

The three judges in the very front raised their cards, giving me an 8, 7, and 9. I guess that wasn't too bad.

"Those should all be tens!" yelled Tiny.

"You thought the last girl should have had all tens too," shouted the guy sitting two rows behind him.

"Because they should!" Tiny yelled back.

"Oh, blow it out your…" started the guy behind him.

"How about I shut you up?"

"I wish you…" The man stopped talking the moment Tiny stood up.

"Not bad. Not bad," said the announcer before turning to me, though I had a feeling that he just said that to make me feel better. "What do you do for a living?"

I swallowed a lump in my throat. "I work at the Candle Shoppe while attending the local university."

The announcer feigned interest, but I assumed he did that with every contestant. "Mellow Summers. That name seems familiar."

Here we go.

"I remember reading about a Mellow Summers in some article. That wouldn't happen to be…"

"Fraud!" shouted the same man that had been arguing with Tiny moments before.

I squinted as I looked out at the audience, doing my best to make out the shadows sitting in their seats, despite the bright lights that shone in my eyes. As I watched, I noticed two of Tiny's men sit on each side of the rude man, who silenced himself and squirmed in his seat as he eyed them both.

"That is in the past," I said, not wanting to talk about Jillian Modsen's scathing articles about me.

A loud cough echoed over the crowd and emanated from Tiny's direction, a clear indication that this line of questioning was to end.

"And so it is," said the announcer, getting the hint. "Mellow Summers everyone!"

I walked off the stage amidst a series of applause, most of which came from Tiny's corner. As I strolled past the judges, I noticed the sour and bored looks on their faces and got an idea. There was just one thing I needed to know first.

"Well, that couldn't have gone any worse," said Jackie as I left the stage. "The nerve of that idiot, bringing up that…"

"Jackie," I said, cutting her off, "do you know where the judges go when they aren't out there watching the contestants?"

"No, why?"

I cursed under my breath, watching my idea disappear, but needn't have worried because a few seconds later one of the other contestants must have overheard us and answered my question.

"They go to room 102 when they're not here."

"Really?" I asked.

"Yeah. It's got all sorts of beverages and snacks for them, the kind that we're not supposed to eat."

"Thanks," I said.

She smiled and walked off, heading for the stage to wait for her number to be called.

I looked at Jackie, getting an idea and rushed back to the changing room to get my cell phone.

"What are you doing?" Jackie demanded.

"I need to get into that room," I told her. "Can you keep an eye out for me?"

Jackie nodded and headed back to the door to watch for anyone that might be coming down the hall.

I dialed Greg's number. He answered on the first ring. "Mel, you were great!"

I smiled, flattered at how he always tried to make me feel better, even though I didn't care about the judges' scores.

"Tiny, almost threw that guy out of here," said Greg.

"I'm surprised that they didn't try to throw him out."

"They did, but changed their minds when he and the others stood up, daring security to do something."

I chuckled at that. Most people rethought their decision to tell Tiny what to do. "I need a favor," I said, remembering why I had called Greg. "Do you have your Bluetooth earpiece with you?"

"Yeah. Why?"

"It's rumored that Melanie was blackmailing the judges and when I was on stage just now, they looked really glum. Almost like they were bored or had already made up their minds about who would win the competition. There is a room they go to in between contests and I want to listen in on them when they think they can speak freely."

"Good idea. I'll bring it to you."

Therein lay the problem. Men, especially boyfriends,

aren't allowed on the floor near the contestants. "You'll have to let Elise bring it. They have rules and…"

"I get the picture. You'll have it in ten minutes."

"Okay. Have her meet me by the vending machines near the stairs. Love ya."

We hung up and I hurried to the door, snatching a robe I saw hanging on a chair.

"So?" asked Jackie.

"Elise is going to bring me Greg's Bluetooth earpiece. Can you go back to the auditorium and let me know when the judges are on their way back?"

"Can do."

We parted ways and I headed for the main floor where the vending machines were kept, ducking behind them, hoping that no one saw me. I paced back and forth, peeking out from behind the candy machine, growing impatient, even though it had only been three minutes. By the seventh time I had glanced around the machine, a blonde mass of hair appeared, startling me.

"It's just me," said Elise. "Here." She handed me the earpiece.

"Thanks," I told her, taking it. "I really appreciate it."

"No problem. Spying on people, that's up Tiny's ally. He's always down for doing anything shady and somewhat illegal."

I laughed a little, knowing how true her statement was. He had helped me break into someone's apartment once just to learn who had murdered a woman during the Christmas parade a few years ago. I thanked her again before running off, sneaking up the stairs to the first floor and creeping down the hallway to room 102. I turned the knob. To my surprise, it opened. I had expected the door to be locked, but won't argue with it being unlocked. I opened it and snuck inside, closing the door so that if anyone walked past they would not see me or be inclined to ask questions.

A long table sat in the room next to the wall on my right, filled with platters of donuts, fruit, and mini sandwiches. Towards one end of the table rested a large pitcher of water with lemons in it and an iced tea dispenser. So, maybe they weren't eating well, but at least they had something to munch on. The contestants weren't allowed to eat anything and many frowned on you if you snuck in a snack, which reminded me that I had a candy bar in my purse.

My phone buzzed. Glancing at it, I saw a text from Jackie. *They're coming.*

Crap!

I took the earpiece and paired it with my phone before opening the recording function, making sure that it worked. I heard footsteps. Spotting a vase with flowers in it, I placed my phone in it, covering it with the flowers as best I could and hurried into the hallway where I hid behind a trash can while I waited for the people approaching to disappear. I watched as the judges stomped down the carpeted hallway and went into the room reserved for them. Placing the earpiece in my ear, I listened as they got something to eat and started to talk. It didn't take long for the conversation to turn towards Melanie Sanders and her mysterious death.

"You might want to go easy on that," said one.

"Shut up," spat the one the first judge talked to.

"What are we supposed to do now?" asked the third.

"Our jobs," said the second, and I thought I had detected a note of sarcasm.

"We've always done our jobs," said the first judge, his annoyed tone coming through clearly.

The second judge snorted. "Not since that Sanders girl managed to snap a picture of you caught in an embarrassing embrace with her."

"How was I supposed to know that she had a camera hidden?"

"What were you doing with her in the first place?"

"Stop it, you two!" yelled the third judge. "Our main concern now is to make certain that the police don't find out. If they do, they might think that we had something to do with it."

"Considering we all had motive," muttered the first judge.

"What's that supposed to mean?" said the second, her tone dark.

The first judge laughed. "Like you don't know. She had evidence that you two were involved in an illicit affair. Something your spouses, or the sponsors of this competition, would not be happy about."

"Don't you…" began the second judge, but the first one just laughed even harder.

"Or you'll what? You'll kill me? How do we know that you didn't have a hand in Miss Sanders' death?"

Before either of the others could respond, my phone vibrated.

"What was that?" asked one.

Uh-oh. They heard it.

It buzzed again.

"I think it came from over here."

I looked around, trying to figure out what to do next. I couldn't just leave my phone there, but at the same time, I didn't want to get caught. I decided to just leave and worry about getting my phone later. Too bad that fate, in the name of Tammy, had other ideas. I turned to leave and there she was.

"Mel! Geez, I have been looking everywhere for you. I can't believe that the judges gave you such bad scores."

I backed away, trying to shush her, but she just kept talking.

"I mean, the nerve of them, acting like they know everything."

"They are the judges for a reason."

"Why are you whispering?"

I glanced at the door, hoping no one came out. "Tammy, now isn't a good time."

"Are you spying on someone?"

"Perhaps we should go," I urged her, but all hints were lost on her.

"Why didn't you invite me?"

Really? Let's just think about that for a minute. Why would I invite someone who talks louder than the participants at a football game to come with me when I'm trying to eavesdrop? "Can we talk about this later?"

The door to room 102 opened.

"What's going on here," demanded one of the judges, storming up to me.

"Nothing," I replied, pulling the earpiece out of my ear and palming it.

"Is this yours?" he held up my phone.

"How dare you accuse her of something!" Tammy shouted back.

This was starting to get a little out of hand, but before I could pull Tammy away, Detective Shorts showed up—with great timing as usual—and put a stop to the entire exchange.

"Mr. Costas," he said, ignoring me and Tammy, "I need you to come with me."

"I'm not going anywhere with you."

Detective Shorts held up his phone, displaying a picture of the judge in a lover's embrace with Melanie Sanders. "We can talk about this here, if you want."

Mr. Costas relented and went with the officers accompanying the detective, handing him the phone.

"And you two," he said to the other two judges.

Knowing their secret was out, the other two judges went with him as well, not bothering to put up a fight.

I tried to sneak away, but should have known better.

"Miss Summers, what is this?" he asked, holding up my phone.

"A smartphone," I replied, receiving a glare in response, indicating that he did not appreciate my sarcastic response. "Okay, I was spying on them. It turns out that Melanie was blackmailing them. She had something on all three of them!"

"I know," said Detective Shorts and I stopped talking. "Unlike you, I am a real detective and we found this image posted on one of those file sharing accounts under Melanie Sanders' name."

"Oh." I hung my head.

"I know you mean well"—he handed me my phone—"but, please, stay out of this."

"Yes, sir."

"Though, that was creative," Detective Shorts said as he walked away, "using the Bluetooth to eavesdrop."

I watched him leave and knew I had to get back to the changing room so that I could put my own clothes back on.

"So, are you going to stay out of it?" asked Tammy.

No. Not that I was going to tell her that.

Left alone with Tammy, I headed back to the changing room to find my clothes and get out of this bikini. Tammy followed close behind like a lost puppy, going on about what had just happened and coming up with one wild theory after another about their connection to Melanie Sanders and how they had gotten rid of her to preserve their reputations. I just rolled my eyes, releasing a nondescript "uh-huh" whenever she mentioned my name.

When we reached the changing room, I found my things and grabbed them. Tammy still followed behind me, talking nonstop. I don't think she even realized that we had reached the vanity room. "Tammy," I said, stopping her, "I'm going to change."

"What about the next round?" Tammy asked.

"The judges just got arrested," I reminded her. Well, they weren't really arrested, just taken in for questioning, but my statement sounded better and made my point.

"Oh," she said, her voice lowering.

I found a privacy screen and stepped behind it with my clothes, wondering where Jackie had gone off to, unless she had decided to change and get out of here. Heaving a huge sigh, and feeling exhausted all of the sudden, I plopped my jeans over the screen and yanked off the bikini top and kicked off the heels. My feet thanked me. I had just snatched my shirt and pulled it on when something sparkly caught my eye. Peeking around the screen, I spotted a couple of other girls who had decided to change like I had, and noticed that Tammy had disappeared. Good. I did not want anyone paying attention to me right then. I pulled on my own undies and jeans, throwing the swimsuit back in its garment bag, not caring if it got wrinkled, and hurried over in my bare feet to the corner, where I saw something shimmer, which also happened to be near where Ruth had found me looking at the application with her name on it.

Some laughter forced me to pause, but the others who were in the room with me hadn't noticed my presence and remained focused on something else. I knelt down and grabbed what had gotten my attention, noting that it was a shoe with at least a three-inch heel and adorned in an array of fake jewels that all caught the light in a manner that made it look more expensive than it was. I guess in this business putting on a good show was more important than having the most expensive outfit. I inspected the shoe and spotted a little bit of mud on the heel, scraping some of the dried soil off the end of the heel itself with my fingernail. Though a big part of me wondered if these shoes belonged to the murderer, my rational mind reminded me that a lot of girls had shoes on while in the park and might have some mud caked on them as well. This wasn't solid evidence of anything. Though, I could get some.

I searched for anything that could be used to transport a sample of the mud, finding some plastic that had once wrapped a few makeup brushes. I snatched it, unfolding it with care, and scrapped some of the caked mud into its center. A bunch of voices filled the hallway. My time was limited. Once I got what I could, I folded the plastic up and shoved it in my pocket, before placing the shoe back where I had gotten it from and darted away. I had just reached the privacy screen when the other contestants burst into the room.

"I can't believe they are cancelling this whole thing," said an irate Candace. "And I'm sure it is all her fault." She pointed at me.

"Back off!" shouted Jackie, pushing her way in front of Candace.

"Or you'll what."

Jackie clenched her fists, but before she could carry out what she wished to do, a harsh whistle rang through the room, silencing everyone.

"Ladies!" shouted the stage manager. "The rest of tonight's event is cancelled. However"—she raised her voice when murmurs raced through the crowd—"we will resume this competition tomorrow at five o'clock. That means everyone needs to be here no later than four, but preferably by three. No exceptions!"

The stage manager stalked out. I thought I saw her share a look with one of the contestants, but it happened so fast that I couldn't be certain and Jackie found me before I could ponder it any further.

"Where'd you go?" I asked.

"Talking with some of the girls here," said Jackie.

"Did you learn anything."

She shook her head. "Unfortunately, no. Most of the girls here keep to themselves. It seems that everyone here is looked upon as competition, so no one wants to become besties."

I blew some hair out of my face in frustration.

"It's okay," soothed Jackie. "We'll figure something out."

"I might be ahead of you there." I pulled out the plastic wrapped mud sample. "I found this on a pair of shoes over there by that vanity."

"Do you know whose vanity that is?" asked Jackie.

I shook my head.

"I'm on it."

"Here," I handed her the keys to her car. "I'm going to catch a ride with Greg. Besides, I'm going to need Jack's help with this mud sample."

Chapter 10

Greg and I pulled up in front of Jack's apartment building. Tiny parked right behind us. We had decided to ask him along, since I had a feeling that Jack would not be too happy to see us, considering, he never was. His apartment was on the first floor, for which I was thankful, because I did not want to have to climb up a bunch of stairs.

Greg knocked on the door.

No one answered. I didn't even hear any sound coming from inside.

Greg knocked again with the same result.

"Maybe he isn't home?" I suggested.

"Oh, he's home," Greg said. "He's just hoping we'll go away." He reached up above the doorway, feeling for something.

"What are you doing?" I asked.

"I know where he keeps the spare key."

Seemed like an obvious place to me. Jack might want to reconsider where he keeps the spare key.

Greg found the key and opened the door, letting both me and Tiny inside. At first, the apartment looked empty and I, once again, thought that perhaps Jack was not home, except his computer was on and the game that he had been playing was set to pause.

"So, where is he? 'asked Tiny, sticking to the shadows.

"He's around," replied Greg.

We searched around the deceptive apartment, but Jack managed to stay well-hidden until…

A slight crunch sounded.

We all stopped, looking for the source, but Greg motioned for us to be silent. He crept over to a set of bookshelves. In a flurry of movement, Greg reached behind the shelves and seized the person hiding there, pulling Jack out into the open amidst a series of protests and cursing.

"You got me, all right! Now, let me go!"

Greg released Jack.

"Can't you people respect a person's privacy?"

"Maybe you should make sure that no one else knows where you keep the spare key," replied Greg, handing Jack the key to his apartment.

"What do you want?" demanded Jack.

I pulled the soil sample from my pocket and handed it to him. "I need to know if this matches the mud down in the sewer."

"I don't have access to that sort of equipment," protested Jack.

"But you work in the building where the lab is located," Greg said.

Jack glared at him. "It wouldn't work anyway. I would need an actual sample from the sewers."

I knew I had forgotten something. I did not want to go back down there, but if he couldn't complete his task without…

"Then, I suggest that you go get some," said Greg.

"I'm not going down into the sewers," Jack said.

"Mel did," Greg countered, receiving a chuckle from Jack.

At that moment, Tiny stepped out of the shadows and into the light of the only lit lamp in the room. "We're going for a ride."

Jack's face fell. He started to open his mouth to protest, but reconsidered his options and clamped his mouth shut, hanging his head and walking out the door with Tiny right behind him. "I hate you," he muttered to Greg as he walked past.

"You know," I said, after Jack and Tiny had left, "we're going to have to make this up to him."

"I know. But, for now, I say we go home."

Chapter 11

I walked into work the next morning, yawning and carrying a cup of coffee that I had only taken a few sips from since getting it from the café down the street. Though I had managed to get to sleep last night, I felt as though I had only gotten three hours instead of seven. Jackie was off today (lucky her) so it would be just me and Tammy. I stifled another yawn.

Dragging myself to the back room where we kept our belongings, I took a drink from my coffee, willing myself to wake up. It rarely worked. My body tended to have a mind of its own, ignoring anything I wanted to do. I put my purse in my locker and went back out to the main store area with my beverage, downing it, hoping the caffeine would kick in. I didn't see Tammy, but knew she had to be somewhere. She usually was nearby.

My phone binged and I checked it, opening the message from Greg.

Jack says that the people Detective Shorts took in last night were released. Alibis checked out. And the soil samples matched.

I put my phone back in my pocket and huffed. Figures that they were released. Even I knew it was a longshot, but now I felt as though I had wasted my time trying to listen in on their conversation. Though they had motive, none of them looked as though they would have risked their careers over killing Melanie. Discrediting her would have been easier. The soil samples matched, though. Did that mean that Ruth had murdered her own contestant? The problem with that theory is that there didn't seem to be a motive for it. According to her, they had decided to part ways. It was a mutual agreement.

A shadow loomed outside the door to the store and I remembered that I had not unlocked it to let people in. I hurried to the door, popped the lock, and opened it. Two elderly women walked in, thanking me, sounding more cheerful than I felt. One of them looked familiar, but it took several moments for me to realize that she was the same librarian who had helped me locate some information on Melanie's past. Why is it I never seemed to remember her right away? Not to mention that this was her second trip to the Candle Shoppe in a week, which was a bit odd because I didn't remember her ever being a regular customer. Did she suddenly decide that she liked candles and wax warmers? I brushed my wandering thoughts aside and welcomed the two women, before heading back over to the cash register to grab the inventory book and look it over.

I couldn't think about the numbers in the book. Knowing I shouldn't, but unable to help myself, I pulled out my phone and typed "Melanie Sanders pageant winner" into the internet search bar. Right away, several results popped up. A few were just bloggers who had decided to put in their two cents about how she died. One seemed promising. I tapped the link.

Local Teenager Wins Local Pageant

Melanie Sanders has been awarded first place in the local Arts in the Park pageant. Known for sporting a scarf that always matches her outfits, it might seem surprising that this young woman has won, but she doesn't see it that way.

"This is just the start of a promising career," she said, when interviewed. "Being a descendent of the Beaumonts, I'm not surprised I won."

A descendant of the Beaumonts? With old blood like that in her veins, it's not surprising that she won. We wish you luck, Miss Sanders. Or should I say Beaumont?

"Have you gone to this pageant that is being hosted?" the woman from the library asked her companion, pulling me from my phone and forcing me to put it back in my pocket.
"No, I haven't" replied the woman.
"Well, you didn't hear it from me, but I heard that the

girl who died in the park, that her dress wasn't even the one she was supposed to wear that day. It had been replaced."

Replaced? I glanced in their direction.

"Yes," said the woman from the library. "Somehow, the outfit she was supposed to wear got something spilled on it."

The two women meandered to the section where our dried herbs were kept that could be burned as incense. I grabbed the inventory book and moved to the area where the two women were, pretending to be counting the items on the shelves and recording their numbers on the pages of my little book, while I listened to them talk.

"Accidentally?" asked the companion.

"Supposedly. But you know how these pageants are."

"But the police said her death was accidental."

"But, then, why are they still investigating it?"

My thoughts exactly. I moved a little closer, still pretending to be writing in my little book.

"Poor dear. Oh! But what if she had been... murdered? What about the other girls in this new contest. Wouldn't they be in danger?"

"I hope not," said the woman from the library. "I just think it's odd that her outfit had to be changed at the last minute because the one she was scheduled to wear had gotten damaged."

That was a good point.

"You are in this Miss Belle Pageant," the woman said to me and I snapped my book shut, freezing in place, wishing I was invisible.

"Um... yes," I replied.

"What made you join such a cutthroat competition?" asked the companion.

"I did it on a lark. Just something to do for fun," I said.

She gave me a look that seemed to say that she did not believe me. No surprise. How many people join a beauty contest on a whim?

The woman from the library checked her watch. "Oh, my goodness! I need to get back to work. It was good seeing you both."

I watched her leave, thinking it a bit odd that she had been in the store to begin with. "Your friend seems to really like these pageants," I said to the other woman.

"Oh, she's not my friend."

"Huh?"

"I never saw her before this morning. She just showed up and started talking to me. Seemed friendly enough."

Never saw her before?

"Oh, where do you keep your centerpieces?" asked the woman.

I pointed at the section where we kept some of our fancier candle holders that held flowers, decorative fare, as well as candles, making pleasant pieces that could add a bit of atmosphere to any room or dining table. The woman thanked me and headed over there, leaving me to wonder what had just happened. Before I could ponder the matter any further I heard a *PSSSSST!*

I turned in its direction and found a pair of frightened eyes staring at me from behind the door to the bathroom. "Tammy?"

She waved me over in a frantic motion.

"What's—YIKES!"

She covered my mouth and yanked me into the bathroom,

locking the door, while fiddling with a head scarf in an attempt to cover up her hair and hide the atrocity it had become. Atrocity is one way to put it. Her hair had somehow turned from the dull brown that it usually was to a neon orange, so bright that I wished I had my sunglasses to look at it.

"What happened?" I asked.

Tammy wrung her hands, debating whether to tell me or not, but I gave her my best "you better talk" stare and she opened her mouth, not even stopping for a breath. "I thought my hair had been looking a little dull and I wanted to spice it up for the pageant tonight, so I bought some hair dye. We weren't busy, and the bathroom at my place is small, so I decided to try and dye it here. But now… well, look at it! It's orange!"

I bit my lip to keep from laughing. This was so Tammy. She always did something crazy when she wanted to try something new. "Didn't you read the box?" I asked her. The container said that the hair color was orange.

"No."

I shook my head.

"It was on the same shelf as the ones for auburn so I just assumed that it was all the same."

If only Jackie were here. She would just bust out laughing and never stop, something I found difficult not to do myself. Tammy's hair would make the Joker's hair look sane. At least she was ready for Halloween, even though that was a few months away.

"Help me!"

"I can't," I told her.

Tammy looked as though she was about to cry.

"Tammy, I'm sorry, but there is no fixing this. You'll have to wait until your hair grows out enough so that you can cut the orange part out, or until the dye itself washes out."

"But what if it never does? I'll have orange hair for life!"

"It will wash out, though it might take a few weeks."

"A few weeks!" The terror on Tammy's face at the prospect of having orange hair for a month surprised me. "What if I redye it with a different color?"

"That will just make things worse. I know it's not an ideal situation, but you are just going to have to wait until it washes out."

"But what do I do until then?"

I tried to take the scarf from around Tammy's neck, but it seemed to be caught on something.

"You have to remove the pin," she told me.

I found the pin, a fan-shaped piece of silver with a small spike attached to it, one she probably made herself, and unhooked it, allowing me to remove the teal-green scarf. After fiddling with the delicate material a little, I managed to tie it around Tammy's head in a way that made her look as though she had walked out of a 1950s movie set, but it did cover her hair so that the orange wasn't too glaring. "This should help," I said. "Just wear hats for a while."

Tammy smiled and turned to look at herself in the mirror.

I realized that I still held the pin. As a thought entered my mind, I studied the pin, wondering why someone would use it to hold a scarf on and thinking that that I had seen someone do that before. "This is an interesting pin," I said.

"Thanks," replied Tammy, taking it. "One of my first attempts at handmade jewelry."

"Why were you using it to hold on the scarf? Don't most people just tie it or wrap it around themselves?"

"Yeah, but it can work itself loose and fall off. So, I use a pin to keep it secured. Besides, I think it adds a bit of decorative flair."

That same thought kept working its way through my head. "Tammy, how many pictures of the event did you take?"

"Lots."

"May I see them?"

She grabbed her phone from her pocket and pulled up the pictures before handing it to me. I scrolled through them, amazed at how many pictures this woman took, and not just of the July Fourth pageant, but of her everyday life. She must love social media, or live on there like so many others. After a minute passed, I finally reached the ones from a few days ago and slowed down so as not to miss any she might have taken of Melanie Sanders. Found them! As it turned out, Tammy had taken a lot of pictures of the poor woman, more so than I realized. I studied each one as I went from image to image until I found one of her just entering the stage.

"What are you looking for?"

"I'm not sure," I said as I zoomed in on the image as best I could, loving the fact that pictures were digital these days and that Tammy actually had a good camera on her phone. I focused on the scarf she wore, hoping that I might find—There it was! Nestled in the blue material was a pin, but I couldn't make out any detail of it.

Tammy tapped her foot with impatience. "What are you…"

"I think I found something interesting."

"About the case?" Her eyes lit up and all annoyance towards me hogging her phone disappeared.

"Possibly." I texted the photo to myself, so that I would have a copy and handed the phone back to her, after deleting my number from it.

An annoyed rapping on the door reminded me that I needed to get back to work. Before I left the restroom, I texted the photo to Jack with a message: *Can you enhance the area around her neck where the pin is?*

A moment later my phone chirped at me with his response. *Fine.*

I chuckled. Despite Jack's insistence that he never wanted to be bothered with my sleuthing, he never did turn down a chance to investigate something. I remembered the story that the elderly woman had told about the dresses being switched and again my mind focused on the handler. She could have replaced the outfit with ease and even suggested it. Besides, her evasiveness when she was questioned about that day never sat well with me and I kept wondering if she hid something.

I texted my suspicions to Detective Shorts, knowing what his response would be.

His reply came within seconds. *Miss Summers, I understand you wish to help, but please, I will handle it.*

Yep. I figured he would say something like that.

The knocking at the door sounded again, but more insistent.

"We need to get back out there," I said to Tammy and opened the door, leaving the bathroom and going back out to the main store area, still wondering how the scrap of cloth I found in the sewer fit in to all of this.

Chapter 12

The time to close the Candle Shoppe arrived and so did my mad dash to the convention center for another night of beautifying myself for others. I loathed doing it, but reminded myself that this was necessary to solve Melanie Sanders' murder. I pulled into the convention parking lot and found a space near the entrance. Before getting out of my car, I checked my purse to make certain that I had remembered to put my makeup, the stuff Jackie had given me the night before, in there. I had. Thank goodness.

Breathing a sigh of relief that I hadn't forgotten one of the most crucial elements for a contestant in a beauty contest, I ran from my car to the door. People already filed in to find a seat in the auditorium. I rushed past them, hiking up the stairs two at a time, and burst into the room set aside for the contestants to use. Glares came my direction the moment I stepped through the door. I wandered over to my station, feeling their eyes follow me as sweat formed under my collar from their unwanted stares.

"Well, there she is."

I recognized the voice. Candace walked up to me with a fake smile as I sat down. "Can I help you?" I asked.

"Not likely. Especially if your way of helping people is to get them fired."

The reason for the stares hit me. Word about the judges being arrested must have gotten around along with my role in it. "Unless there is something you want, I suggest you leave," I said, growing tired of this woman and her snide remarks each time I ran into her.

"You know, it's not just the judges who were fired," said Candace.

I gave her a questioning look.

"It seems that someone also let slip to the police that Melanie and her handler didn't get along. Police also found a torn dress and muddy shoes in her things. She was arrested this morning."

"I had nothing to do with that," I said.

"Just like you had nothing to do with the judges being replaced?"

I glared at her.

"Funny thing, though, Melanie never wore orange."

"Leave me alone."

"And just what are you going to do about it?" Candace challenged.

Soon after she had said that, a squirt of purple liquid

shot at her, staining her white blazer and spilling onto the rose-pink blouse she wore underneath.

"Look at what you did!" she screamed at me, but I hadn't done anything.

Tammy appeared by my side dressed in snakeskin pants, a taupe-colored shirt with so many frills that it appeared to be in constant motion, and a bandana made from cloth flowers that disguised her orange hair well. "Go pick on someone else!"

Candace opened her mouth to speak, but snapped it closed the moment Tammy held her grape juice box in front of her ready to fire off another shot if provoked. "Fine," she snapped.

"Really, Candace," said another woman, "haven't you caused enough trouble?"

"What do you mean?" challenged Candace.

The other woman crossed her arms. "We all know why Melanie had to suddenly change her outfit."

Some of the other girls had gathered around us and my attention turned from Candace being annoying to wanting to know more about what this woman had to say.

"That was an accident!" yelled Candace.

"No, it wasn't," said someone else. "We all saw you. You spilled your water on her outfit on purpose."

"I'm not going sit here and let myself be—"

"Ladies!" The stage manager entered, cutting Candace off and forcing the other women to split up. "You're on in fifteen!"

I rushed in, putting powder on my face to calm the oiliness that had developed.

"Number thirty-eight!"

Man, that woman's voice was annoying. No wonder they had made her the stage manager. She had a voice that got anyone's attention. I turned and watched as she rolled a cart over to me.

"These are the outfits that have been designated for you to wear. You'll find your choice of casual wear for the next event, cocktail dresses, and formal wear for the final event tomorrow. If anything doesn't fit, just let any of the tailors or myself know."

I nodded and she stalked off, clutching her tablet as she scrolled through the night's scheduled events. Across the way, I noticed the woman who had come to Tammy's and my aid. "Excuse me," I said to Tammy as I stood up and went over to the woman.

The woman busied herself with finishing her outfit for the next round, turning in front of the mirror as she compared two different sweaters.

"Pardon me," I said to her.

"Yes?"

"I wanted to thank you for helping me out back there."

"It's no trouble. Candace never did like competition."

"I'm Mel."

"Amy."

A speck of gold caught my eye and I looked down, spotting a pair of dress sandals with sequins on the straps, making them sparkle with the slightest amount of light. I picked them up. "These are pretty," I said, rubbing some dirt from my finger and thumb, "but they're a little dirty."

"Oh, I know," replied Amy. "I wore those in the park. Even though the grass was dry, heels tend to sink into

the soil. I had forgotten those were there with everything going on. I'm not the only one who had a pair of
shoes ruined by it either." She reached for the shoes and
I handed them to her.

"A bit disappointing."

"You don't know the half of it. These aren't even
mine." She looked at the number printed on the bottom
of the shoe. "These are size six and I wear sevens."

"How did they get here?" I asked.

"Things get scrambled around here," replied Amy.
She reached for a pair of red, open-strapped shoes with a
heel that made me cringe and put them on her pedicured
feet. "You might want to get dressed."

"Amy!"

We both jerked and found the irate stage manager
standing behind us.

"You're on," the stage manager said in a gentler tone
when she noticed our startled faces. "But before that, a
Detective here wants to speak with you."

"A bit demanding," I muttered when she left and
Amy laughed.

"I guess it goes with the territory of managing a
beauty pageant." She stood up and took a few steps, tripping on her fourth one.

"Are you okay?" I asked.

Amy laughed. "Yes. I never was very adept at walking
in heels, but that also goes with the territory."

I knew I should get back to my station and get changed,
but I had one more question to ask to satisfy my curiosity.
"Why are you here? This doesn't seem like your thing."

"That first prize will go a long way towards paying for college. Even the prize for second place could help with some bills."

"Twenty-one!"

"Got to go."

When Amy hurried away, her awkward strides a clear indicator of her not being used to walking in high heels, I thought I saw the stage manager scold her, but couldn't tell amidst the crowd of other contestants parading around in their casual wear. After a minute, Amy disappeared into the hallway where the distinctive shape of Detective Shorts waited for her and they both disappeared. The call for another contestant reminded me that I needed to get ready.

I hurried to the cart that had been brought for me and riffled through it, looking for ideas on what to pair with what, wishing Jackie were here. Where was she, anyway? I never saw her in the room. Knowing I was out of time, I snatched a pair of red capris, a blue ruffle blouse, and an ivory jacket. A bit patriotic, but since July Fourth was a few days ago, I figured it would fit. After I had changed, I did my best to apply eyeliner, having never been a pro at it, and hoped it looked passable. The room emptied even more as I touched up my blush, eye shadow, and lipstick.

"Come on! Last call!"

The stage manager's voice forced me out of my chair and I hopped around as I put on the shoes loaned to me. More heels. Those seemed to be the only kind of shoes allowed in this place. As I struggled with the strap of one, I fell down. When I sat up, I spotted a burnt orange dress, hiding on a cart of evening wear which was tucked away in a corner near the door. I raced to my purse and pulled out the scrap of cloth I had found and hurried back to the cart where the dress was. Ignoring everything around me, I held the material up to the jagged edge of the gown and they matched.

"Thirty-eight!"

I jumped and dropped the cloth.

"You need to get out there now!" the stage manager hissed at me.

"But…" I started to say, but she hauled me to my feet and pushed me out into the hallway in front of a few other contestants who all watched us with interest.

"Why is it, none of you girls can get out on that stage on time?" She continued to usher me towards the stage entrance, never giving me a chance to speak. "I do not get paid enough for this!"

Before I knew it, I was thrust into a line with other contestants and forced onto the stage, unable to stop them. Jackie stood in her spot, waiting her turn.

"What happened?" she mouthed to me, but before I could answer her, she was called on stage.

Within seconds it was my turn. For the second time in my life, I found myself strolling onto the stage amidst a few cheers, applause, and an announcer speaking into the microphone with such enthusiasm that I wished he would pass some of it to me. The blinding lights caused me to squint a little as I walked underneath them, sweating from their heat and nerves.

"Number thirty-eight, everyone!" said the announcer.

I went to the edge of the stage and twirled, following Jackie's example from earlier, showing off my outfit and feminine curves.

"She is sporting a very patriotic fare with her chosen colors, perfect for a July Fourth weekend, though I could see anyone wearing that blazer any day of the year."

The announcer waved me over to him and I stopped my spin and stood by his said, waiting for the judges scores. I tried to see their faces, but couldn't make out much. Though, I could tell by their different body shapes that the judges were different from the night before, not that it was much of a secret. The showrunners had already sent out notices of the change. I watched as they held up their score cards: 9, 10, 9. Well, at least they were better than last night.

"They should all be tens!" Tiny's voice carried over the noise of the audience.

"Dude," said someone else, "you thought the same thing last night. Maybe she is—"

I just imagined how the person speaking chose to stop the moment Tiny turned and glared at him.

"Not bad. Not bad. Give it up for thirty-eight!" the announcer, said, ignoring the momentary outburst within the audience as he waved his hand to the other end of the stage and I knew it was time for me to leave.

I tore off the blazer the moment I left the dais since I had been boiling under those stage lights. How do people do this on a constant basis? Jackie found me within seconds.

"Mel!"

"Where have you been?" I asked her.

"Here. Backstage," she replied. "Sorry I wasn't there when you arrived, but I wanted a chance to try and make friends with some of the contestants."

"And?"

"There isn't much, but Candace is the reason for Melanie's dress being ruined that day, forcing her to use a different one."

"Actually, someone told me that while I was changing."

"But what you don't know, is that it was Melanie's handler that had bumped into Candace in the first place, causing her to spill her water. Some of the girls talked about how it looked like it had been on purpose."

"Why would Melanie's handler do that?"

"Good question," said Jackie.

A series of applause from the auditorium reminded us that we needed to change for the next round, which started in an hour.

"Come on," said Jackie. "We need to do something about your hair for the cocktail round."

We hurried back to the changing room. The area bustled about with furious activity as the other girls changed into their cocktail dresses and touched up their makeup. As Jackie rushed to the cart of outfits that had been brought to my vanity station for me to use, I paused by Amy's vanity, looking at photo of two teenage girls that I hadn't noticed before. The image seemed dated, but I could tell that one of the girls within it was Amy since the jawlines matched. The two within the photo smiled, relishing a joyous moment—a snapshot of a happier, simpler time. I leaned closer, trying to see what was pinned to their jackets.

"Mel!" hissed Jackie, interrupting me.

I jerked my head in her direction and allowed her insistent hand to wave me over. "Sorry."

Jackie searched through the dresses, shifting one after the other to the side, her face frowning with each one she looked at.

"I'm sure any dress will do," I said.

"You don't understand," replied Jackie. "If you don't get high scores in this round, then you won't be allowed to participate in the final round, which means you'll be banned from coming back here."

I hadn't thought about that. The scores never bothered me, but having Jackie remind me of the only reason I was allowed back here in the first place, made me nervous that I hadn't done well.

"This ought to do." Jackie held out a deep purple, strapless dress that fell just above my knees. A small bow decorated the top hem, centered between the breasts which added elegance without drawing attention to the bust.

She handed me the dress and I stepped behind a screen to change, having to suck in my stomach to be able to zip it closed, another reminder that I needed to hit the gym. The silky material felt cool against my skin and I admired myself in one of the mirrors as I stepped out so that Jackie could scrutinize me.

"It goes perfect with your hair," she said, "and speaking of your hair..." She ushered me into a chair and fussed over my tresses, using a wide curling iron to put in loose curls that draped around my face.

"It's a little tight," I told her, commenting on the dress.

"You'll live. Besides, you're not going to be wearing it for long."

True, but I hated feeling as though I couldn't breathe. I chose to not focus on how tight the garb was around the middle. What else was I going to wear?

"There you go," said Jackie, pleased with what she had done with my hair. "You're all set."

She ran off to her own station to touch up her make-up and put on the cocktail dress she had picked out for herself earlier, a silver piece of art with bits of red woven into the hemline giving it a bit of a flirty flair.

"I need you all backstage now!" yelled the stage manager, storming through the changing room in her usual no non-sense and grumpy manner. The groans that filled the room told me that I wasn't the only one who found her annoying.

Before I jumped out of my seat to join the line of con-testants fleeing the room, I put some lip gloss on to give my lips a little shine, a trick that Jackie had taught me.

"Thirty-eight! Let's try being on time for a change."

The stage manager stood next to me, reminding me of the fact that in every instance she had told me to get on stage, she had to repeat it three times. I turned toward her and saw a tiny, one-ounce bottle of liquid latex stick-ing out of her pocket, but she shoved it back in and urged me to get going. I didn't need to be told twice. The other contestants had already vacated the room and I did not desire being last for a third time.

I joined the line of others as we filed out of the room and to the stage entrance, awaiting our few seconds to shine in the local lime light. One by one, each of the girls were called on stage and shared a few laughs with the announcer. My eyes widened when Tammy went on stage in a dress made from… straws? How did she find the time to do that?

"Is she wearing plastic straws?" I asked Jackie.

"Yeah. She challenged their disqualification from last night, saying that there was nothing in the rules about not bringing or making your own clothing," Jackie whispered to me.

I watched as Tammy paraded on stage in her outfit of multicolored plastic, amazed that it actually looked good, and she wore it well. The dress waved with each movement and Tammy's exuberant smile radiated how pleased she was with her accomplishment. As her time ended, the next girl walked on stage, turning her sour frown into a pleasant smile as though she were happy to be there.

Jackie's turn arrived. I watched as she strolled onto the stage. She spun around a couple of times, showcasing her petite curves, exhibiting perfection as she did not even look as though she wore makeup and not a strand of hair stood out of place. If she didn't attain high scores, then this contest was definitely fixed.

"Number thirty-eight!"

Oh no. My turn. I pasted a smile on my face and walked out, sweating the moment the bright lights touched my skin. Following the example of those who had gone before me, I turned around a couple of times, allowing them to see me in my purple dress and showcasing how well it fit, despite the fact that I had a little difficulty breathing.

"Well, Miss Summers, that is quite the outfit. Very classy, indeed. Where did you get it?"

As though he didn't know. "You know I can't tell you that," I teased, thinking it was best to play his little game. "That is a woman's secret."

He laughed and I wondered if the audience noted how fake it sounded. "Ten, nine, and ten. Very nice scores."

I watched as a bulky shadow moved behind the judge that held up the nine and sat behind him, and guessed that it was Tiny. The poor judge lowered his arm a bit as a nervous expression crossed his face. Knowing I had to leave, I walked off stage and headed back to the changing room, wanting more than anything to get out of this dress.

A ping and a buzz filled my ears as I entered the room and I rushed over to my purse where my phone was. I pulled it out and brought up the message. It was from Jack. He had enhanced the photo I had asked him about. My phone chirped at me again followed by a buzz. This time it was Greg.

Detective Shorts just arrested Melanie Sanders' handler. Jack just told me. They found evidence that she had poisoned Melanie.

She'd been arrested? I never trusted what she had told me about how she and Melanie had amicably decided to go their separate ways, but did she really commit murder?

I put my phone away and grabbed my clothes, stepping behind the screen and changing back into something sensible. According to Greg, they had found evidence of her poisoning her own contestant. Maybe she did do it. A yawn worked its way to the surface and I realized that I needed to get home and get some sleep. I put the cocktail dress and shoes away before finding Jackie and leaving the convention center with her.

Chapter 13

I woke up from a deep sleep, my mind still wondering why the second girl in the photo I had seen near Amy's station looked familiar. Seven in the morning. The sun only just peeked through the shade of my window, the first reminder that the time to get up had arrived. I sat up, pushing my long hair out of my face, not wanting to know what it looked like, though I could guess. Why did that girl look so familiar?

A copy of the book by the local author I had visited two days before lay on my night stand. I picked up the book and flipped through it, looking at some of the pictures, marveling at how people managed to dress in so many layers during the summertime and survive without modern air conditioning. One page had a photo of three women posing for the camera. Their serious faces were a far cry from the selfies and best bud pictures that inundate social media sites. I read the caption underneath the photograph.

The Beverly sisters posing for their first photograph. Septembers 1836

Remembering what little I knew about the history of the camera, I realized that pictures were not instantaneous like they are now, hence why many in those older black and white photos never smiled. The three sisters reminded me of something and, once again, I thought about the photo at Amy's changing station. I knew I had seen it before.

A memory hit me. When I had lunch with Mrs. Sanders, a photograph fell from her wallet and it had been a torn edge. I needed to get to the library. I had a hunch, but I wanted to confirm it. The library opened at eight in the morning and I didn't need to be at work until eleven, so I had time. I dressed in a hurry and rushed from my room to Jackie's, stopping myself when I heard soft snores coming from her room. Maybe I should let her sleep.

Before leaving, I wrote a quick note for her and left it on the coffee maker, knowing she would get it the moment she made her morning cup of coffee. I closed the front door, making certain to not make any noise and turned towards Greg's door, pausing when I started to knock. He would come with me. I knew he would. I decided against it. He had been working late nights for the last few weeks and never got home until three in the morning, after which, he would turn around five hours later to go back to work. His sleep is more important and I was only going to the library.

Within thirty minutes, I pulled into the library's

empty parking lot. Few people came here this early, which was good because that meant I wouldn't have to wait to use the microfiche machines or look through the books of older newspaper articles. I hurried downstairs where the machines were kept. Upon opening the door to the archive room, I found the same elderly woman whom I seemed to have kept running into all week. The odd moment passed as I reminded myself why I was there.

"May I help you, dear?" she asked, looking over the top of her reading glasses.

"I need to use your microfiche machine to look up some older newspaper articles," I replied.

"Just sign right here," she said, handing me a clip board with a paper on it where you sign your name and the time you checked in. "Is there a specific set of articles you are interested in?"

I thought for a moment as I signed my name and put the time down. Most of the contestants were in their late teens or early twenties. The girls in the picture looked to be at least sixteen, maybe a year or two younger. "Starting in 2011 to today."

The woman nodded and walked over to a set of shelves. "These are all of the local articles starting from January 2011."

"I'm surprised that these aren't all online," I said, making conversation.

"I'm sure they will be put on that internet, as you all call it, but for now, they are all collected down here and put into book form. I make sure that the library special orders each issue of the local paper like this. I'm surprised

that you didn't try to look this up on… the web? Most
don't come down here anymore to do research."

I tried to do most of my local research on the internet, but sometimes you find an article in the search results, but when you click on it, you are told that you need
a subscription to view it, something I found annoying. I
didn't tell her that. "Not everything is available online."

"Well, these should help you get started." She headed
back to her desk. "That is a nice shirt by the way."

"Thank you."

"That color reminds me of a pageant that took place
a couple of years ago. All of the contestants had to wear
these matching orange dresses and gold sandals. It was
lovely. They stood in formation and sang *America the
Beautiful*. Talk about a wonderful performance. Unfortunately, some of the girls failed to return their dresses to
the company that had loaned them out. Ever since, our
local pageants have not been as spectacular, or well-done.
Well, I best let you get to work. Listen to me go on, like
a crazy old lady!"

I didn't care if she did keep talking. I had never paid
much attention to local events, and she just gave me
an interesting bit of information. I opened my mouth
to ask a question, but she had disappeared quicker than
I thought possible for one her age. Thinking better of
chasing her down, I turned back to the giant books of
every newspaper issue from the last six years. I started
with the first one.

Even though it was only six years old, the pages had
yellowed some, a sign that the humidity control in this

room did not always work, or that fingers of several people had touched them. I flipped through the large pages, taking my time in perusing the headlines, but found
nothing. When I reached the end of the first book, I
paused, rethinking my strategy. What if these news articles only covered the town I lived in?

The shuffling of loose leaf papers caught my attention
and I watched as the woman read through what appeared
to be forms. I walked over to her. "Excuse me," I said,
knocking on the door to the small office, "but do you have
any news articles that cover the surrounding towns?"

"You have everything you need right there," she replied. "Those books contain every newspaper for the entire county for the last six years, just like you asked."

I gaped at her. I know I had asked about the dates,
but didn't remember inquiring if they covered the entire
surrounding area.

"You'll find what you're looking for."

Knowing I had been dismissed, I went back to the
table I had been at and grabbed the next book of newspaper articles on the nearby shelf. I plopped the book
on the table, cringing when it made a thud. The elderly
woman never looked up from her forms. One by one, I
turned the pages, scanning the headlines and images, but
found nothing. By the time I had reached the third book,
three hours had gone by. I looked at the clock, wondering if I was going to find what I searched for. Growing
frustrated, I turned the pages of the third book with less
enthusiasm, thinking that perhaps I should call it quits.

A familiar face stared back at me. I stopped and flattened

the page, smoothing it out. The same picture of two girls, like what was at Amy's station, stared back at me, except this one had three girls in it. All of them hugged one another and each possessed a huge smile as though they had just had the best day of their life. I glanced through the article.

Tragic Accident Kills Local Teen

In the early hours of this morning, a tragic accident claimed the life of a local teen. Wendy Wilson, the teenager killed in the accident, was a senior at Southwest High School and looked forward to graduating in five months. Unfortunately, that will never happen now.

"She had such a kind heart," remembered one classmate of hers.

It was believed that she was on her way home after attending a party in which alcohol was involved. An investigation is being conducted and one of the other teenagers involved in the accident is being detained, though prosecutors have not yet decided if they are going to pursue involuntary manslaughter charges.

Wendy is survived by her parents and two sisters.

So, Amy had a sister who had been killed. Though this doesn't prove anything, it is interesting. I studied the picture and realized that the third girl matched the same torn photograph that had fallen out of Mrs. Sanders' purse. What had she said? That Melanie and her closest friend had a fight? Why didn't she just mention this incident? The more I thought about it, the more I concluded that Mrs. Sanders did not want to relive a tragedy and she had just lost her daughter. Perhaps she figured that it wasn't important. Or, maybe, she didn't know all the details herself. She had said that she hadn't spoken to her daughter since she left home.

I checked the time and realized that I had been at the library for three and a half hours and I needed to get to work. I grabbed the book to put it away, but it fell from my grasp and opened to a page different from the one it had been on. At first, I started to close the book, but stopped when I noticed an image of Amy holding a trophy, but looking somber.

Teen Survivor of Tragic Car Crash Wins First!

Senior Amy Wilson can be seen proudly holding the trophy for first place in the 800-yard run at the last track meet of the school year. It comes with a somber note since her sister, Wendy, cannot be here with her. Only a year apart, the two had been very close and had planned to compete together.

Wendy Wilson had tragically died in a car accident

five months earlier. Though she was a year younger than her sister Amy, Wendy had been skipped a year after having tested out of her junior level classes. This moment was supposed to be a triumphant one for both, but remains a bitter reminder of where one fatal choice can lead.

"We had hoped to graduate together," said a tearful Amy. "But now all I have are painful memories."

Amy Wilson has been a talented track star since her freshman year and her sister Wendy could always been seen sitting in the stands supporting her. This would have been Wendy's first year running track.

"We had planned to do some extracurricular activities together since this was our last year in high school. She agreed to take track if I agreed to join the drama club."

Though the community celebrates in Amy's success, they also mourn for her loss.

She ran track?

I pulled out my phone and texted Jackie. *Is it possible for someone to run in heels and cover a great distance in a short amount of time?*

You know it is, replied Jackie.

What if the same person had run track in high school and only graduated a few years ago?

My phone chirped with Jackie's reply. *I'd say it's definitely possible, then. What have you found?*

I checked the clock in the room and knew I had to get going. *Tell you later*, I messaged her back and put the book of news articles back on the shelf.

"Thank you," I said, poking my head into the small office of the archive room, but the woman had gone. A little confused, but unconcerned, I left and ran upstairs. She must have had to go to the restroom or something.

My hand still clutched my phone as I ran upstairs and the idea that Greg might be able to get Jack to help me, entered my mind. I sent him a text. *Found some interesting stuff about one of the contestants. Can you get Jack to find out more information about an Amy Wilson?*

No problem.

I smiled. He was too good to me sometimes. I raced up the stairs and out the library doors to my car. I had just enough time to swing by a fast food place for some lunch before going to work.

Chapter 14

The time for the last round in the pageant had arrived and like the other contestants, I bustled about trying to get my evening gown on, dreading wearing those high heels again. I admired myself in one of the floor length mirrors that they had provided, remarking at how well the dress fit.

"Here," said Jackie, handing me some glittery, rose-colored lip gloss and some purple eyeshadow that sparkled in the light.

"I already have makeup," I told her.

"Yeah, but this will help make you stand out."

I took the lip gloss and eyeshadow, applying it just like I knew Jackie wanted me to. I had to admit that the eye shadow did make my eyes pop and the lip gloss showed up better under all the lights than what I had been wearing. "Thank you," I said.

"So, what did you find out at the library?"

In all that had been going on, I hadn't had time to talk to Jackie about my discovery and work had been so busy today that we didn't get even a few minutes to talk. Also, Tammy had called out, saying she had some emergency, or something. We didn't care. Mr. Stilton allows us some time off throughout the year for illnesses and this was the first time Tammy had taken a sick day.

"Something interesting about one of our contestants," I said. "I asked Greg to have Jack double check some info for me and if I'm right, I might know what happened to Melanie."

Just then, Tammy ran into the room, carrying an outfit that clinked with every movement and reflected the light around it. Both Jackie and I gaped at her, trying to figure out what it was she had brought.

"I need some help," Tammy said to us when she reached us.

"What is that?" asked Jackie.

"My dress for tonight."

"Why don't you use one of the ones they provided?" continued Jackie.

"The theme is most original evening wear," replied Tammy. "So, I brought this. I made it myself. It took over six months, but I managed to finish it up today."

Jackie and I both gawked at the gown as Tammy unfolded it and held it up. It had been made out of bottle caps and possessed a single strap that went over the left shoulder to help hold it up. Accompanying it was a belt made out of copper pennies, which complemented her orange hair and her shoes—I have no idea how she had done it—had been created from decorative brooches. The entire outfit, though unusual, looked elegant and impressive.

"Um… yeah, we'll help you," said Jackie, impressed by what Tammy had made.

We led her over to a more secluded area of the room and pulled a changing screen over so she could undress. Jackie grabbed the bottle cap dress and looked it over, trying to figure out how to undo it. "Is there a zipper on this thing?"

"I used hooks and eyes," replied Tammy. "Couldn't fit a zipper into it."

Jackie reexamined the back of the dress and found the way to undo it.

"What is that atrocity?" asked a snide voice and I knew who had said it without having to turn around.

"Go away," Jackie hissed at Candace.

"You can't seriously be thinking that you will win in that," Candace continued.

Jackie positioned her foot so that bottom of her heel snagged on Candace's dress and ripped it the moment she moved.

"Look at what you did!"

"Do you want me to rip it some more?" Jackie's nose remained an inch from Candace's. I had never seen her so angry before, but Candace must have struck her final nerve. Jackie may have found Tammy annoying, but she loathed Candace even more. "At least she tried to come up with an original design whereas your rag looks store-bought."

Candace stalked off in a huff, heading straight for her cart of clothes, pulling one dress off a hanger after another, tossing them aside.

Pleased that Candace had left, Jackie barked at Tammy to turn around and held the bottle cap dress as she stepped into it. We both fastened the hooks and eyes and I marveled at how the unique gown looked every bit as fantastic as some of the ones you find in those boutique stores. I wondered why she couldn't have made all her ostentatious outfits look this elegant. Once we had her dress fasted, Jackie wrapped the copper penny belt around Tammy's waist, which added a bit of colorful flair to it.

"Shoes," said Jackie.

I snatched the handmade heels and paused as I stared at the various pins that they were made of. The pins. I thought back to the photo of Amy, her sister, and Melanie. Only Amy and her sister wore pins—matching pins. Melanie hadn't worn one at all.

"Mel?"

"Here," I handed Jackie the shoes and hurried back over to where my purse was, pulling my phone out of it. I pulled up the image that I had Jack send to me earlier. Just like I thought. It was the same pin, but Melanie hadn't owned one like that.

"Last call, girls!" yelled the stage manager in her usual crass manner.

As the girls lined up, I meandered over to Amy's station.

"Now, remember, girls. This time, you will be asked to perform a talent as you show off you evening wear creation."

I looked at my dress and frowned. I just used one of

the ones provided for me. Some of the girls had done the same, some had purchased an evening gown and modified it some, while others had sewn something unique to them.

"Come on!" yelled the stage manager. "Back stage. Now!"

The contestants filed out of the room and I watched as Jackie helped Tammy walk in her heels. I hung by Amy's station and when everyone had left, I made my move. I opened drawers and riffled through the powder compacts, cosmetic bags, jewelry, and even a cup full of pens, but found nothing. Growing frustrated, I feared that I would continue to find nothing. I swiped my hand across a shelf that held hair accessories when a familiar object fell on the table in front of me. The same pin as in the photograph. I picked it up.

My phone rang and I answered it.

"Mel?" It was Greg.

"Hey!" I greeted him.

"I just left Jack's and will be at the convention center in five minutes."

"What did you learn?"

"You need to get out of there."

"What?" I asked, wanting to know, more than ever, what Greg had learned.

"Get Jackie and Tammy and get out!"

"Greg, what's wrong?" I moved towards my purse and wondered how I was going to get Jackie and Tammy.

"Jack confirmed that Amy had been a track star. She ran both cross country and track while in middle school and high school. After she graduated, she started entering local beauty pageants. And here's the other thing, it turns out that Amy's sister, Wendy, was killed in a drunk driving accident and Melanie Sanders was in the car with her. The D.A. dropped all charges of involuntary manslaughter, and kept her name out of the press out of consideration for the family, when it was confirmed that Wendy had been driving and Melanie's blood alcohol level was below the legal imit. She went through the windshield and died. Melanie only suffered minor injuries. The most she got charged with was underage drinking, but juvenile records are sealed upon your eighteenth birthday."

"But there is no way Amy could have done everything on her own if she is guilty. She had already crossed the stage when Melanie had died. And she has been backstage or on stage like the other contestants when the shoes and dress was discovered in Ruth's things," I said.

That's it! Amy might be involved, but she couldn't be in two places at once. And none of the other contestants could have done it since they were also backstage. But the person who planted those items, who poisoned Melanie, had to have access to everything and who would always be entering the changing area.

"Mel, are you listening to me?"

I just realized that my wandering thoughts had prevented me from hearing Greg's last bit of news. "What?"

"Amy has another sister."

"What?" I said again. "Who?"

"She has a sister who is twelve years older than her. Clara Olgerstein."

"Who?'

"Your stage manager," said Greg.

The stage manager? Of course!

"Clara's maiden name is Wilson."

"Greg, I have to go," I said. "Make sure that Tiny and the others are in the auditorium. I'm going to get Jackie and Tammy now."

I heard a rustling just outside the room. Clutching my phone and the pin, I snuck out into the hallway, unsure of what I would find. It was Ruth. "What are you doing?" I asked.

She glared at me. "Oh, it's you. Can't you just leave me alone? Haven't you done enough?

"What do you mean?"

"Like I don't know that you're the one who called in that tip and placed those articles of clothing in my box of things."

"I didn't—"

"Look, I'm just here to get the last of my stuff. Just go away."

I started to leave, but stopped, remembering what I had read about ricin. "Did Melanie eat or drink anything right before the pageant that day?"

Ruth released an annoyed sigh. "Most of the contestants have restricted diets. Melanie said that she felt a little unsteady and I know she wasn't eating properly. So, I asked someone to get me some orange juice."

One dose of ricin wouldn't be enough to kill someone, especially if home brewed. But what if she had been receiving doses of it for several days or weeks.

"How many of these contests did Melanie do in a year?" I asked.

"There is a local one almost every month and they

mostly have the same faces. The contestants rarely change. You and your friends are the only new ones here."

I watched as Ruth grabbed a box with various brooches in it. "Did Melanie always wear a brooch? Just seems like an odd thing to wear in a contest like this."

"Usually, yes. It was the only way to ensure her scarves never fell from her neck. But that day, I couldn't find them."

"Couldn't find them?"

"This box had disappeared. I must have misplaced it. Strange how it showed up now?"

"Then, where did you find the pin that she did wear?" I asked.

"Clara gave it to her to borrow. Are you done?"

"Yes," I replied, turning back into the room, unaware of the time. How would anyone be giving Melanie regular doses of the poison without her knowledge? A pitcher of water sat on a table in front of me. I glanced around. On every vanity table was a pitcher of water and a glass. I had never paid much attention to it before, but it occurred to me that water would have to made readily available to the contestants at every pageant, otherwise the participants would get dehydrated.

"Thirty-eight!"

I jumped. Clara, the stage manager, stood behind me.

"You are going to be the end of me. Why can't you ever be where you are supposed to be?" She noticed my phone and snatched it from me. "Making calls? It can't wait?"

Sweat formed on my forehead as I fumbled for words. I had just been about to open my mouth to speak when she saw the pin in my other hand. Words were not needed. I knew she recognized it. Fearing what she would do, I shoved her into a table and ran out of the room, darting down the hallway as best I could, but the heels I wore proved to be a hinderance. I tore them off and dropped them as I ran. Pounding footsteps echoed behind me and I knew Clara was close behind. I headed for the stage entrance, hoping to find shelter among a crowd.

I burst through the door to the back of the theater and hurried towards the entrance, and tiptoed onto the stage, taking my place in line with the other girls who all stood poised in the lights, waiting their turn. Clara stopped and glowered at me from the sidelines.

A few of the other girls gave me odd glances as I snuck on stage and I'm certain that my bare feet attracted questions. I looked ahead of me and watched as Jackie finished with the announcer and went back to her place in formation.

"Thank you, thirty-seven," said the announcer. "Hello thirty-eight! Miss Summers!"

Taking my cue, and buying myself some time, I walked over to the front of the stage, my bare feet leaving soft plops on the smooth floor while the hem of my gown brushed the top of them.

"Why, you seem to be missing your shoes!"

I grinned at the announcer and chuckled, formulating a plan. "It appears so."

"Are you going to grace us with a bit of ballet like one of your fellow contestants had earlier?"

"No," I replied. "Instead, I am going to regale you all with a story." I looked over the audience, hoping that Greg and Tiny were there. I thought I saw the familiar shape of Detective Shorts. Had he been attending every round?

"A story!"

"Yes," I said in a sweet voice. "A tale of intrigue, mystery, and murder."

"Well, do go on."

I took a deep breath and began. "About four years ago, two teenagers had decided to go to a party. Of course, there was alcohol involved and they stayed out late into the night. Instead of taking a bus or calling a cab, they decided to drive home and got in a car accident. The driver died, while the passenger lived."

I glanced at Clara and Amy, whose expressions had changed.

"The sister of the driver, her name is Amy, mourned and grieved for months, even running a race in her sibling's honor. But the driver had another sister, Clara, and though there was a least a decade between them, she loved her siblings very much. A few years later, when the two learned that the other girl in the car had joined and won some local pageants, all of that grief and the feeling that justice had never been served resurfaced. They let their anger brew, until they concocted a plan.

"Clara taught Amy what to do and how to act, helping her get into a few pageants until she had built a reputation, while she herself, managed to get hired as one of the backstage coordinators. No one suspected that they were siblings because of the age difference and the fact that they do not share the same last name."

Murmurs grew within the crowd and I knew I had to be quick.

"Amy had changed her appearance so that when she and Melanie had met, she was not recognized. Either that, or the two had silently agreed to pretend not to know each other. Now that she had gotten herself in the same set of pageants that Melanie was in, both Amy and Clara could put their plan of revenge into action. It started small. First, Amy would drop ricin into the pitcher of water at Melanie's station as she walked past it to get to her own. It wasn't difficult. The other contestants cared more about themselves and ricin is easy to make at home. It is easy enough to grow castor beans and with the help of the internet, one can learn how to make ricin from them.

"Homemade ricin is never as potent as the stuff made in a laboratory, so, Melanie did not die right away. Instead, she thought she had the flu as she experienced the symptoms of vomiting and nausea. But over time, the poison built up in her system until she died from it."

"No!" yelled Amy. "She wasn't supposed to die!"

So that answered that question. I continued my tale as Clara snuck away from the sidelines. "It all came to a head on July Fourth. Though Amy was content with just making Melanie ill, Clara wanted her dead. She timed her entrance into the changing area so that when she walked in, she was able to trip Melanie's handler, who, in turn, bumped into one of the other contestants, who had been carrying some water, forcing her to spill it all over Melanie's dress. This forced her to put on another one, one that had been placed on her cart by Clara hours before. Knowing that Melanie always wore a scarf to hide a scar on her neck, left there by the accident, Clara made sure she had a pin ready to lend to her, after having hidden the ones that Melanie normally used. But this pin had been soaked in a more pure form of ricin as Clara had been perfecting her skills at making the poison. After having lined her hands in liquid latex for protection, she even volunteered to help Melanie secure the scarf, making certain not to prick herself, but she did pierce the skin of Melanie. This added to what had been building in her system for weeks, ensured her death."

"She didn't mean to!" Amy yelled in disbelief.

At that moment, Detective Shorts headed for the stage.

"Amy recognized the pin on the scarf, since she and her deceased sister had matching ones. So, she grabbed the scarf and the pin during the commotion and left the stage, squeezing though the broken grate to the sewer. Being a former track star, it wasn't difficult for her to run through the culvert, but she couldn't get through the bramble that tore her dress and was forced to turn back. Clara had seen her sister disappear, and stopped her at the nearest manhole, convincing her to come back up. Amy did and Clara gave her a pair of shoes to change into. No one noticed the tear in her dress since all of their attention was on Melanie."

Security came onto the stage and headed straight for Amy.

"She wasn't supposed to die! She was just supposed to be sick for a while!" Amy cried as she was escorted away. "Clara, you promised me."

A tremendous crash echoed from backstage and Clara rushed out into the bright lights. She took one look at security and ran for the steps that lead into the audience. I watched as she raced for the exit, running below us. Out of nowhere, Tammy ran barefoot to the edge of the stage, jumped, and tackled Clara, pinning her to the floor. Clara tried to get away, but by the time she got Tammy off her, security and Detective Shorts had reached them both.

"Guess you didn't need me after all!" came Tiny's voice from within the crowd.

"Dude, your talent sucked!" yelled a familiar voice.

"How about I show you some of my talents?" Tiny threatened him, receiving a warning glare from Detective Shorts.

Once Clara and Any had been led away, the curtain lowered and we were told to wait until the police told us we could leave. Jackie found me and gave me a hug. "How did you figure it out?" she asked.

"Luck and a lot of guesswork. How did you like Tammy's tackle?"

"I will never think of her the same."

We both shared a laugh as we waited to be questioned by the police over the night's recent events. I hoped they finished soon. I really just wanted to go home.

Chapter 15

I welcomed the joyous sounds of people eating a meal as Greg and I sat in a local diner the next morning. We had decided to meet for breakfast now that the chaos of the pageant and the arrests of Amy and Clara had calmed and withered away. It was nice being able to sit down and enjoy a meal.

"So, Amy really didn't want to murder Melanie?" I said.

"According to Jack, she really did just want to make her sick for a while. It was Clara who decided to take it further."

"How did he find this out?" I asked, already knowing the answer.

"Same way he helps us half the time."

"Amy must have panicked when she realized what Clara had done. Even though she knew her actions would make her an accessory, she still tried to protect her."

"Well," said Greg over a mouthful of egg, "she had already lost one sister. I guess she just didn't want to lose another."

"I'm glad it's over. I'm not sure how much longer I could take putting on globs of makeup and parading in heels."

"But you were sexy when you did."

I laughed.

"How did Jackie take the announcement of the winner?" asked Greg.

After the police had finished interviewing all of the contestants and stage hands, the judges decided to announce the winner of the Miss Belle Pageant: Tammy.

"She said that Tammy deserved it," I replied.

"Really?"

"Yes. According to Jackie, Tammy did have the most original outfit."

"I'm sure jumping off stage and tackling a murderer helped," Greg chuckled.

I checked the clock on my phone, having forgotten to put on my watch. "I need to get to work. See you later tonight?"

"Deal."

I picked up the check and paid as I left the diner, giving Greg a final wave as I headed for my car. Before heading to the Candle Shoppe, I stopped by the library first, wanting to thank the elderly woman who had helped me in my research. She seemed to do just about everything there and it only seemed proper to thank her. I arrived at the library a few minutes later and hurried inside.

"May I help you?" asked a different woman at the circulation desk.

"Yes," I replied. "I wondered if you could help me. I'm

trying to find someone who worked here. She's older, gray hair in a bun, wears reading glasses."

The librarian just stared at me as I had just described almost every employee there.

Exhaling, I tried to think of how I could give a better description when I noticed a black and white photograph hanging in a corner. I had never noticed it before, but started to get a weird feeling as I studied it. "That's her," I said, pointing at the image.

The librarian laughed. "That's impossible."

"But she's the one I want to see. I want to thank her for helping me the last several days."

"Look, I don't have time for someone's idea of a joke. There is no way you talked to her."

"Why's that?" I asked.

"If I have to hear one more time how she has been seen… According to some, the woman practically lived here. She was one of the first librarians to work here."

I gave her a confused look.

"She has been dead for over forty years." The librarian rolled her eyes at me and walked off, muttering to herself.

I inched closer to the photograph and read the date on it: Mrs. Abigail Templeton, 1976. Realizing that this was the second time I had met a ghost and not known it, I left the library. As I reached the exit, I glanced over at a table where a student studied the pages of a book and standing next to him was the same elderly woman that had assisted me. She smiled and waved before disappearing. I shook my head, smiling to myself, and left.

Look for book 14 in the series

Hey Diddle Diddle The Zombie In The Middle

About the Author

Janet McNulty currently lives in West Virginia where she continues to work on the Mellow Summers Series. She began the series two years ago as a fluke, but liked writing it so much, that she decided to stick with it.

Besides writing paranormal mysteries, Ms. McNulty has also accomplished success in other genres. She has a fantasy saga (*Legends Lost*) published under the name of Nova Rose and a new dystopian trilogy (*Dystopia*) and acience fiction series (*Solaris Saga*) as well. Ms. McNulty once referred to herself as an author who is "a little something for everyone."

She is currently busy working on the next Mellow Summers book.

Of course, writing is not the only passion in her life and every author needs some down time. When she isn't working on her books, Ms. McNulty enjoys reading and just poking around in her garden.

More by Janet McNulty

The Mellow Summers Series

Sugar And Spice And Not So Nice
Frogs, Snails, And A Lot Of Wails
An Apple A Day Keeps Murder Away
Three Little Ghosts
Oh Holy Ghost
Where Trouble Roams
Two Ghosts Haunt A Grove
Trick Or Treat Or Murder
Roses Are Red…He's Dead
Double, Double, Nothing But Trouble
Ring Around The Rosy, Not Another Ghosty
Hickory Dickory Dock The Ghost In The Clock

Violets Are Blue More Trouble Brews

Mellow Summers moves to Vermont to attend college, accompanied by her friend Jackie. They soon find themselves running into ghosts and one mystery after another.

The Solaris Saga

Also available in audio.

Solaris Seethes
Solaris Seeks
Solaris Strays
Solaris Soars

Every myth has a beginning.

After escaping the destruction of her home planet, Lanyr, with the help of the mysterious Solaris, Rynah must put her faith in an ancient legend. Never one to believe in stories and legends, she is forced to follow the ancient tales of her people: tales that also seem to predict her current situation.

Forced to unite with four unlikely heroes from an unknown planet (the philosopher, the warrior, the lover, the inventor) in order to save the Lanyran people, Rynah and Solaris embark on an adventure that will shatter everything Rynah once believed.

The Legends Lost Series

Published under Nova Rose

Tesnayr
Amborese
Galdin

Enter the Lands of Tesnayr and join on an epic fantasy adventure that spans over 1,500 years.

Begin with Tesnayr, the first king of the five lands as he unites the against a savage foe bent on their destruction.

Next, Join Amborese as she fights reclaim the throne after her family was forced to flee from it.

Thinking peace has finally entered the land, follow Galdin as he returns to Tesnayr to find it greatly hanged. Barbarians, led by a mysterious sorcerer, burn and destroy as they go. And only Galdin can stop them if he chooses to accept his fate.

Visit www.legendslosttrilogy.com to learn more about the Legends Lost Trilogy.

The Dystopia Trilogy

Dystopia (Book 1)
Tempered Steel (Book 2)
Liberty's Torch (Book 3)

*Also available
in audio.*

Imagine living in a world where everything you do is controlled.

Dana Ginary lives in a world where every aspect of her life is controlled by the Dystopian Government. Forced to work in Waste Management, her life becomes a nightmare with hunger and survival is her only constant. Before she knows it, she is caught up in a resistance movement and exiled from Dystopia, forced to find her way in the barren wastelands. While there, she must learn to live independently and discover how far she is willing to go to live and achieve freedom.

Something for the Little Ones

The Dragon Who series

The Dragon Who was Afraid of the Dark
The Dragon Who Went to the Moon
The Dragon Who Found a Monster Party
The Dragon Who Found a Spider in His Shoe
The Dragon Who Explored the Sea
The Dragon Who Caught a Cold

The Fairy Who series

The Fairy Who Lost a Tooth
The Fairy Who Got Lost

Mr. Chili's Chili
Mr. Chili Goes To School
Mr. Chili's Halloween
Mr. Chili's Christmas

Others:

Mrs. Duck and the Dragon
The Hungry Washing Machine
Rhymes-a-lot
Are You the Monster Under My Bed?
How Do You Catch An Alien

Grandpa's Stories

My grandfather grew up in Arizona during the 1920s and 1930s. One week after the attack on Pearl Harbor he joined the Navy. During the summer of 2012, my mother visited him and recorded his stories about growing up, World War II, and his time as an employee at the Pacific Bell Telephone Company. This is the history of the 20th century as he lived it. These recordings make up this book. These are his words.